TEE-BO
The Persnickety Prowler

FINDING THE STOLEN BOX

"There, I've got it!" Cam said and began crawling backward on the log. "Look!" he whispered, when he was standing on the damp sand with Carlyle and Tee-Bo once more. "It's a little chest. It was in a waterproof sack of some sort, but I took it out and let the sack down in the water again. It sure was heavy."

"That's the box!" Tee-Bo said, his whiskers trembling. "Good boy, Cam! Now, let's—"

He stopped, and for a half second there was a terrible silence. The children looked up. Before them loomed the unmoving figure of a man, his arms, legs, and head all shadowy and dark.

"It's Scoop!" cried Tee-Bo, and, with a tremendous leap, he jumped straight at the shadowy figure, a fierce growl gurgling in his throat.

"Run for it!" he cried as he fell back to the ground and leaped again. "I'll fight him off! Run!"

TEE-BO
THE INCREDIBLE TALKING DOG
on the trail of
THE PERSNICKETY PROWLER

by Mary Burg Whitcomb

illustrated by David K. Stone

cover by Olindo Giacomini

GOLDEN PRESS
Western Publishing Company, Inc.
Racine, Wisconsin

CONTENTS

1 What Happened on the Stairs   11

2 Trouble at the Cottage   27

3 A Very Thin Man   38

4 A New Friend   48

5 The Robber Again   60

6 Behind the Bookcase   75

7 What Was Hidden in the River   86

8 A Desperate Plight   93

9 The Plight Worsens   106

10 The Real Racer   116

11 The Contents of the Box   128

1

What Happened on the Stairs

If anyone could tell you how many stairs there were from the cottage to the beach, it would be the children. They counted them the first time they went down and again when they went up. A level stretch of deep, white sand led from the very door of the cottage to where the beach began to slope down to the river, but it was bordered by a screen of willows that permitted only the upper half of the mountains to be seen. As soon as one had walked a short space, the row of trees ended, and there, in full view, lay the fifty-three stairs and the high, white mound of the beach and the sunlit river streaming by, glinting invitingly.

The summer resort town was named Monte Rio, "mountain of the river," while the stream itself was one of California's earliest named: the Russian River.

On the day this story begins, the children—Cameron, who was eleven, and his sister, Carlyle, who was a year younger—were walking up the stairs. They were taking their time, hopping here and stopping there, engrossed in conversation and not bothering to count the stairs at all. They had been up and down so many times this vacation that they knew almost every splinter and every loose board. Halfway up, they both stopped.

"Here's where we saw the lizard yesterday," Cameron said, bending over to look through a crack.

"And Tee-Bo had to scare it away," his sister added.

"He could have caught it easily."

"He never catches anything," she said. "He just chases things for the fun of it. I'd hate it if he killed things, like some dogs do. Look, here he comes!"

A black and white dog had darted out of the bushes up ahead and was coming toward them in a shower of dust, the stairs shuddering under his bouncing feet. When he reached their step, the children patted him vigorously, pulling out burrs and foxtails as he first shook dust all over them, then caressed them with his rough tongue.

"You never catch anything, do you, boy?" Cameron asked, running his fingers through the dog's thick coat.

"Father says you couldn't even catch cold," Carlyle giggled, pushing the dog down as he leaped altogether too joyously against her.

"He's good at hiding things, though, aren't you, Tee-Bo? Huh, boy, huh?"

The children grinned at each other.

"It was sort of strange, wasn't it, Cam," remarked Carlyle, "when Father was so upset and said, 'That pesky dog'—"

"He said *critter*," interrupted Cam.

"*Critter*, then. Anyway, he said, 'That pesky critter didn't have sense enough to take *two* tennis shoes but took only one, as if he expected me to wear just one shoe,' and the next time Father looked, the other shoe was gone, too!"

"Smart dog," said Cam. He wiped his hand across his forehead, leaving a streak of dust behind. "It's hot."

Carlyle looked soberly at the bushes that lined each side of the broad stairs. "I wish those berries were good to eat."

Her brother frowned. "They're dusty."

"The dust would brush off."

The children stared at the bushes, not saying a word. Suddenly everything became quiet, a strange sort of quiet, just the way it is at a concert when the maestro lifts his baton to begin the first note— or when somebody hears the principal's footsteps in the corridor outside the schoolroom—or when Father says, "Where is tonight's paper?"

Even Tee-Bo was still. His tail stood straight out behind him, and he quivered, his eyes on the bushes.

"Mother said they're thimbleberries," Carlyle said dreamily.

A haze was settling over the sky, as though a summer cloud were floating by, veiling the sun. For a moment, the children felt quite cool.

The bushes were heavy with round, tightly packed fruit resembling large raspberries, only not so red, since they were powdered with dust.

"I think I'll taste one," Carlyle said. She reached out and picked the nearest berry. Cam watched without a word while she put the fruit to her lips. The red juice splashed on the white of her teeth as she bit into it.

"It tastes like a cobweb at first," she admitted, "but then it's sweet. Want one?" She pulled off a second berry and handed it to her brother, watching with great curiosity as he bit into it.

Cameron swallowed, then nodded. "They *are* sweet. I like raspberries better, though."

"These are only thimbleberries," Carlyle said. "That's a funny name. I wonder why they call them thimbleberries."

"Forevermore!" a strange voice said right in their ears. "If you'd brushed off the dust first, you would have seen that they look just like Mother's thimble. But, naturally, you had to eat them, dust and all!"

At first the children went rigid. Then they moved their heads around slowly, but no one was there. Tee-Bo, on the stair beside them, was panting a little, his red tongue hanging out and his eyes curiously alert.

"Who . . . who said that?" Cam asked, his voice thin.

Carly stared back at him. "I didn't," she whispered, beginning to shiver.

"Well, somebody said it!" declared Cam, but not very loudly.

"*I* said it, naturally!" The same voice came to their ears again, this time sounding rather vexed. "But since neither of you has ever been able to hear me, I *don't* see what's troubling you."

It was certainly an odd voice—not a grown-up's and not a child's but somewhere in between—and it had a strangely familiar ring to it that made the children stare at each other, their mouths fallen open in astonishment.

"Whatever is the matter with you two?" the voice

went on. "Those berries are harmless; you can't be poisoned. Let's go home, my dear children."

Tee-Bo stretched his jaws and snapped at a passing gnat, this time missing. "I'll teach those pesky critters to dine on *me*," the voice said.

"Carly," Cam said in a shaky whisper, "I think it's Tee-Bo we hear."

"Nonsense," the voice replied briskly. "You can't hear me talk. That's absurd."

"We can too, Tee-Bo," said Carlyle. "We can hear you as plain as day!"

The dog turned around on the stair, making a circle, then sank back on his haunches, staring at them. His chin whiskers trembled in agitation. "Forevermore!" he breathed, disbelief in every syllable.

For a moment, the three surveyed one another in silence.

"Say something else," Cam said slowly.

Tee-Bo swallowed and then coughed.

"Please say something, Tee-Bo," Carly begged.

"I feel too self-conscious," the dog began, lifting one paw to scratch and then hastily dropping it. Then he sneezed several times, turning his head aside with a comical look of apology. "I'm . . . I'm not sure," he went on, "if *I* should boast or if *you* should—or if we should all go somewhere and hide. It's very confusing."

"Confusing!" Carlyle's voice rose almost to a

shriek. "I think it's most stupendously magnificent! Oh, Tee-Bo," she cried, putting her hands on either side of his furry face and staring into it, "you can really talk!"

"Please don't scream," the dog said hastily. "My eyesight is not too good, but my hearing is extraordinary. I'm not bragging, you understand. It's just a simple fact."

Cam was still staring, his mouth hanging open. The dog looked at him anxiously.

"There's a gnat buzzing about you," he told the boy. "Couldn't you snap at it or something?"

Cam's lips closed abruptly.

"I guess we're all a little shaken up, boy," the dog said, his tone worried.

"I didn't dream you could talk, Tee-Bo," Cam said then. "Who taught you?"

"My mother." The dog sighed, still eyeing them carefully. "Are we all right now? All of us?"

"I still think I'm dreaming," Carlyle confessed, "but it's the best dream I've ever had. Talk some more, Tee-Bo."

Tee-Bo regarded them silently, and then his mouth opened. His chin whiskers began to quiver, and his furry sides rippled.

"What's the matter?" asked Cam. "What are you doing?"

"I'm laughing," replied the dog. "I never thought

anyone would have to ask *me* to talk. My mother used to call me a chatterbox."

"But why couldn't we hear you before?" pursued the boy. "Are you sure you've always been able to talk? I've never heard you."

"Boy," returned the dog carefully, "not only have I been talking all my life, but, among my friends, I also have a reputation for being quite well educated. Of course, not every dog has the advantage of living with a family whose father is a history professor and whose mother is an angel. I consider myself quite fortunate."

Carlyle stared at him thoughtfully as he spoke. "Tee-Bo," she declared, "you must know everything about us, but we hardly know *anything* about *you.*"

"Then," responded the dog, with a shake of his head, "we shall set to work immediately to get acquainted, and the first thing I would like to say is that I'm extremely thirsty."

"So are we!" the children answered together.

"And," the dog continued, "I also want to tell you that I think it's absolutely *fantastic* the way you two always keep my water bowl full of cold water and *clean*. Forevermore, I've been so grateful to you so many times, my dear children."

At this, Cam scowled and looked embarrassed. "Sometimes Father has to remind me . . . a lot . . .

Tee-Bo. I . . . well, I do forget."

"Me, too," Carly giggled, but then her face changed. "But never again. Now you can ask, can't you, Tee-Bo?"

Cam was still puzzled. "Have you really been talking, just like this, ever since we first knew you?"

"Ever since I was born," Tee-Bo answered, his tail wagging in circles, now that he was more relaxed. "All creatures do."

"Cats, too?" asked Carlyle.

"Uh-huh. Cats, dogs, everything. We all talk. And it's pretty discouraging never to be heard."

"How awful!" Carlyle said, hugging him and laying her cheek against his shaggy face.

"I'm terribly sorry, boy," Cam told him. "If . . . if we shouldn't hear you again, will you holler or something?"

"Or bite our legs," Carlyle suggested. "Bite sort of hard."

"Forevermore," Tee-Bo said, "I've barked, I've nibbled, I've tugged. I've tried a hundred times to tell your parents things—things of great importance, too. But I had to give that up. Your mother, the angel, always fed me, and your father always told me—"

"Yes," Cam interrupted quickly, "we know what Father said."

"That man exasperates me so," Tee-Bo sighed,

"but he's the salt of the earth. Take it from a dog. I know."

The children smiled. It was wonderful to hear Tee-Bo talk, but to hear him compliment Father was the best thing yet.

"Yes, he's the salt of the earth," Tee-Bo said again, and he sat down on the stairs, licking at a bug that crawled nearby and tumbling it down onto the cool sand under the boards. "I seldom eat bugs," he explained. "They make me thirsty."

They began ascending the stairs again, slowly. The cool haze that had come so mysteriously had vanished now, and though the day was ending, the heat lingered.

"What I would like to know," Carlyle said, "is what happened to make us hear you. Why couldn't we hear you before?"

"I always thought it was your ears," said the dog. "They are such flat little things—and immovable."

The children looked at each other's ears, meanwhile feeling their own.

"Our ears haven't changed," they said, puzzled.

"It was probably the berries, then," the dog said with great conviction.

"The berries!" cried the children together.

"Have you eaten them before?" asked the dog, assuming an air of authority, just like a grown-up. They shook their heads.

"I hope they weren't poisonous!" Carlyle whispered uneasily.

"Forevermore," Tee-Bo said, shaking sand from his coat, "I wouldn't let you eat anything poisonous. I can tell the difference, if you can't."

"It must have been those berries," Cam decided, giving the bushes a long look.

"Mother said nobody eats thimbleberries anymore," said Carlyle. "I wonder why not."

"Shouldn't we be going home?" asked Tee-Bo. "The sun's going down, and Father will be calling."

They ran over the cool sand in the shade of the willows and reached the cottage a few moments later. Father, turning the hose over the lawn, saw them coming and waved. Tee-Bo bent his head and, with a scattering of sand, shot off in Father's direction with the speed and fury that he usually saved for squirrels. The children began running, too, as the fragrance of the garden reached them, along with a tantalizing aroma floating out the kitchen window. But Tee-Bo, having turned around, met them midway, shaking his wet fur in a shower over both of them.

"Drat the man!" said he. "I wasn't going through the pansy bed! All I did was run through the hose!"

"Did you tell him that?" asked Cam.

"Tell him!" Tee-Bo's brows shot upward, and the curly hairs on the lower end of his jaw trembled.

"Do you suppose *he* can hear me, too?"

"I don't know. We can, but then, we ate the thimbleberries."

Tee-Bo stood there, a picture of consternation. "This could cause complications that would stagger the imagination," he said, after a short silence. "I can see where I am going to have to be somewhat more careful than in the past. You and Carlyle had better go first. If Father heard what I said just now, my chances of dining tonight are nonexistent, and that may hold for the rest of my life."

"Remember, Tee-Bo," Carlyle said anxiously, "you said Father was the salt of the earth."

"Oh, I did, I did," agreed Tee-Bo, "but, take it from me, he has his more peppery moments, too. But run along now, and test his temper for me. I'll lag behind a bit."

The children ran up to their father, who laid one arm across their shoulders while holding the hose in his free hand. Father was tall and rather thin, with rumpled hair. At home, the neighbors thought he looked much more like a sort of tired old football player than a professor of history. Also, he could never really make himself look stern, because he had a friendly kind of face, and the friendliness was always popping out, even when he was gruffest.

"Tee-Bo thinks you're angry with him. Are you, Father?" asked Carlyle.

"Not any angrier than is customary," said their father. "I could just skin him alive is all." His eyes twinkled.

"He didn't mean it," Carlyle called to Tee-Bo, who remained a hose-length away.

"Father," said Cam suddenly, looking worried, "do you ever hear Tee-Bo talking?"

"Constantly," said Father. "He's the greatest gossip and scandalmonger we have in these parts— also the greatest thief. If he doesn't bring back my shoes," he went on, paying no heed to the children's horrified faces, "I'm going to skin him alive. Tuesday, at three."

"Hear! Hear!" called Tee-Bo from across the grass, with the deepest derision.

"That's not nice, Tee-Bo," Carlyle called back, forgetting herself.

"But do you ever really *hear* Tee-Bo talk?" Cam persisted, more serious than ever.

"If that dog could talk," Father said, "he'd tell me where he hid my shoes—I hope—but I might have to squeeze it out of him."

The children looked at each other. It was pretty clear that they alone were able to hear Tee-Bo.

"Carly," said Cam, "let's go get a drink."

"Go in and help Mother," their father called as they fled. "Dinner is nearly ready."

Once around the back of the house, they stopped,

breathless and wide-eyed.

"He can't hear you. Father can't hear you!" Carlyle said excitedly.

"That's pretty obvious," agreed Tee-Bo. "If he could, I'd *really* catch it from him!"

"I don't know just how to tell him about you, Tee-Bo," said Cam.

"Hah!" was the dog's reply. "Tell him, if you wish! He'll never believe you in a month of Sundays. Not him!" His chin whiskers shook more than ever as he spoke.

Carlyle looked thoughtful. "I don't think he would, either."

"But we ought to tell him."

"And Mother, too," Carlyle added, "but she would probably believe us—"

"Or think we had hallucinations, like that time when we were sick."

"I don't remember that," his sister replied, "but we wouldn't want her to worry about us."

Tee-Bo had walked over to the edge of the clearing, where the deep wood began. "Let's not borrow trouble!" he called over his shoulder. "That's what Mother always says. Besides, there's a squirrel over there, just begging me to chase her. I'll be back soon for dinner. *Adios!*"

"Where did he learn Spanish?" asked Cam as they approached the back door.

Carlyle giggled. "He said himself that his friends think he's well educated, and well-educated people speak all kinds of foreign languages."

"Carly"—Cam threw his sister a sidelong glance as he, too, began to snicker—"I think one of Tee-Bo's dog friends is a Mexican Hairless, and *that's* where he learned to say *adios!*"

All but hysterical with raucous appreciation of their own humor, the children lurched into the kitchen, offering, much too late, to help Mother with dinner.

2
Trouble at the Cottage

Dinner was the pleasantest time of the day. It was served on the screened front porch, where they sat at a round table, with the scents of river and forest floating in to them. From across the darkening mountain came the good-night call of the quail and the *too-to-hoo* of the owl, sounding muffled, as if he had buried his beak in his feathers, always answered by another owl, ridges away. The children were quiet and sleepy, burned by sun and cleansed by the river. Mother and Father passed dishes and chatted of this and that.

Suddenly four feet pattered across the floor, and

Tee-Bo came in, tossed a look at the children, and settled down on his favorite corner rug. He yawned loudly and then coughed with great self-importance. "That squirrel!"

"He never fails to show up at mealtime," commented Father, buttering his fourth ear of corn, "looking as though he hadn't eaten for days. Humbug!"

Tee-Bo raised one ear and gave a little sniff.

"You needn't expect me to feed you now, sir," Mother said to him cheerfully. She reached out to cut the pie. It was Blackberry Whipcord, an original recipe of Mother's, and the cooling juices curled red and inviting over the crisp crust. "I daresay *you* don't want any pie," she said to Father.

"Only two small pieces," replied Father, "for now." He leaned back in his chair, sighing luxuriously. "I know you are not a good cook," he said to his wife with great kindness, "but you do serve the most wonderful meals in the world."

Mother looked modest and touched one ear. "It's my golden earrings," she said, though, of course, she wore none.

"No, it's your golden heart," said Father. "A meal cooked with love can't be matched."

At this, Tee-Bo let out his breath with such a noise that even Father looked at him. "No pie for you, light-fingers, until you bring my shoes back."

"Oh, go fly a kite!" Tee-Bo said rudely.

"Tee-Bo!" exclaimed both children.

"Ooops! Scuse me! I forgot you could hear!" said the dog, getting up and shaking himself in deep confusion.

"Tee-Bo, did you take Father's shoes?" Cam asked, without thinking.

"He knows I did," the dog growled.

"Then why don't you bring them back?"

"I'll tell you what happened," said Tee-Bo. "Every morning your mother, that angel, would see those tennis shoes of your father's on the bathroom floor, right where he stepped out of them. Every morning she would say, 'Dear, please don't leave your tennis shoes on the bathroom floor. They'll get wet from the shower.' And they would, and then the way that man would bellow was a caution. So I removed them."

"Children, do you want more pie?" Mother asked for the third time. "I think they're half-asleep," she said to Father.

Father gave them an indulgent look. The children's cheeks were pink and their eyes sleepy. Both heads were turned in the direction of Tee-Bo.

"No," he replied, "they seem to be carrying on a top secret conversation with the more intelligent member of our family, who has clammed up, now that he is under pressure. If Tee-Bo ever breaks under the third degree and tells where he has hidden the loot, in this case merely an unimportant pair of sneakers that I wear—well, *used* to wear—every blessed day, I think it will rain Roquefort cheese."

"Oh, loquacious, loquacious!" murmured Tee-Bo, rolling his eyes. "How we do talk when we're full to the brim with pie!"

Mother had raised her eyebrows at Father's words. "I thought that *you*, my man, were not given to the use of such slang as 'clammed up' and 'loot' and so forth, particularly before the tender ears of your young."

"A perfect angel," murmured Tee-Bo, settling down with a contented groan.

"True," said Father hastily, for slang was outlawed in their household, "but this only goes to prove that I have been driven to dire extremes by this arch-knave, this . . . this depredator, this cat burglar of the canine world."

Tee-Bo surveyed Father with a mournful air. "He certainly knows how to hurt a fellow," he sighed, which unaccountably sent the children off into such gales of laughter that Mother excused them from the table and Father suggested it was time for bed.

The next day they went a little earlier to the beach, for their usual picnic.

"Two weeks more," said Father, carrying Mother's bag, with sunglasses, suntan oil, sandwiches, oranges, and lipstick in it, in one hand and the beach umbrella in the other, "and then back to the slum."

"Yeah," snorted Tee-Bo, running at his heels, "a four-bedroom capitalistic hovel—some slum!"

"I don't know," Father continued, taking great strides and deep breaths. "It might be good to get back to carpets, at that, instead of sand and rocks. Of course, the rest of you have shoes. *I* go barefoot —the master of the house!"

"That does it!" Tee-Bo stopped in his tracks. "I'm going back and get those shoes out. I never heard a man carry on so about a pair of two-ninety-eight tennis shoes!"

"Good boy!" said Cameron. "We'll save you some lunch."

"*Now* where is that dog off to?" said Father, looking back as Tee-Bo made a beeline for the cottage.

"Probably to recover your shoes, dear," said Mother, her face calm and innocent, while the children were speechless with astonishment.

"Do you think Mother can hear Tee-Bo?" Carlyle said when they were settled on the beach and out of earshot.

"No. She just knows Tee-Bo pretty well."

"But maybe *she* ate one of the berries!"

"We should tell her, anyway. And we should tell Father," Cam said, but not very convincingly.

"But we don't know if it was the berries."

"And maybe we'll lose our power to hear Tee-Bo, too. Maybe we won't be able to hear him again— ever."

"If you can hear me now," said a raspy little voice behind them, "listen well, because I have news that will turn your freckles into goose bumps!"

Tee-Bo had returned and stood looking at them as they sat on a blanket under the beach umbrella.

"We can hear you," said Cam. "What happened?"

"I just had a fight with a leg," said the dog, speaking very low and distinctly, as one does when bursting with excitement and self-importance, every curly hair on his chin standing out and quivering, "and this leg was attached to the remainder of a prowler who desired to . . . to *prowl our cottage*, yessir!" He was so excited and out of breath that he had to stop. He lay there looking at them.

"Prowl our cottage! You mean a *burglar?*" asked Cam.

"Well, not yet a burglar; that is, he didn't quite get a chance to burgle. I stopped him. I stopped his leg, and that was quite effective in stopping the rest of him. The leanest, boniest, toughest leg I ever had the . . . the *pleasure* of attacking. Yes, sir!

A pleasure is just what it was!"

"Was he inside the cottage?" demanded Cam, getting excited, too.

"Hah! Inside the cottage!" snorted the dog. "Not quite, I tell you! He was halfway through the back window and pulling himself in, when he found it . . . he found it . . . ah . . . *expedite* to withdraw hastily! Ha-ha-ha! Forevermore!"

"Stop trying to use such big words," Carlyle reproved him, patting him to stop his trembling, "and just tell us what happened."

"I guess it's pretty plain, Carly," Cam said admiringly. "Tee-Bo just stopped a thief from getting into our cottage."

"Oh, when I get mad, I get fierce!" Tee-Bo said, and he curled his upper lip in a dreadful sneer but was simply too exhausted by excitement and his routing of the burglar even to growl.

The children stood up. "Let's tell Father," said Carlyle.

"Wait!" Tee-Bo said. "Get back in the shade again. Think a bit, you two. The thief is gone. I bit him and sent him flying—oh, *did* I!—and how will you explain that to your father and mother? You weren't there. How could you possibly know about it?" He stared at them. "See what I mean?" They nodded. "Now I'll go back and guard the cottage. I won't be able to play or have any fun," he ended plaintively, "but I know my duty, yes, sir!"

While they were eating lunch on the beach, Cameron stopped chewing suddenly, his mouth full of crackers and peanut butter. "Father," he said, "do you and Mother have any valuables in our cottage?"

Father regarded him with polite expectancy. "I think you asked me a question, son," said he, "but it sounded more like the Mongolian national anthem. When did you learn that?"

"Nonsense," said Mother, who could always interpret peanut butter. "Cam asked if we had any valuables up at the cottage, and the answer is no: We're all down here. Excepting, of course," she amended quickly, "your tennis shoes, my dear. But I wouldn't dare to put a price on *them*."

"All our valuables aren't down here," Father objected. "I do have a few rare books that I wouldn't like to part with. Why do you ask, son?"

"Oh"—Cam dug his toes in the sand, embarrassed —"I . . . I wondered if there were any prowlers, ever, at resorts like this."

"I wondered, too," Carlyle said quickly, feeling sorry for her brother.

"I really hadn't thought about it," Mother said, "but I suppose prowlers take vacations, just like other people."

"You mean they rest up from prowling?" Father asked politely.

"Certainly. Prowling is probably boring and . . . and confining."

"And in our humble abode," Father continued oratorically, "no doubt most unrewarding. But, to answer your question, Cam, I think we do not have much that a thief would bother with. My wallet's in my pocket, right here, and Mother has her watch and rings in her purse. All he could steal would be our clothes, and need I add that even a second-rate prowler wouldn't be seen—"

"Prowling in them," Mother finished. "So worry not, old boy." She rumpled Cam's hair and then reached into her bag. "Have an orange. No one can swim for an hour after lunch."

"We don't have *any* valuables?" Cam persisted. "Not even some *little* things?"

"No." Father took out his pipe. "Why? Do you want to brag that we are millionaires traveling incognito? I don't mind; go ahead. You might even mention—casually—a few illustrious ancestors!"

"The rich history professor's children," teased Carlyle, tickling her father's bare back. It was a favorite joke.

"I am now going to sleep," announced Mother, putting on her sunglasses and settling back in her beach chair.

"I am now going to think," said Father, puffing gently on his pipe.

"We are now going to depart," said the children together, this being the last, and their part, of the familiar ritual.

They headed for the fifty-three stairs that led to the cottage.

"Let's find Tee-Bo," Cam proposed, "and see if the prowler came back."

3
A Very Thin Man

When they reached the top of the stairs, Tee-Bo came bounding to meet them.

"He came back, all right!" the dog said, without waiting to be asked. "The same prowler came back!"

"Did you bite him again?"

"He didn't get that close! He just walked by, over near the trees. I let him know what he could expect if he came into the yard again, and he kept a healthy distance!"

"But, Tee-Bo," asked Carlyle, "what does he look like? Is he old?"

"I told you. He's tall and thin."

"So is Father."

"But not bony. And your father doesn't have teeth marks on his leg. This man does. And he's ugly. Wears a real citified suit and walks like this."

Tee-Bo's attempts to walk like a skinny, dandified man in a suit of city clothes made the children laugh so hard that he soon quit, considerably miffed.

"It's no joke," he said sternly, "and, furthermore, it's a real problem to me. I have to stay and guard the place while you play at the beach. Fine vacation I'm having!"

"We'll help you, Tee-Bo," Cam said earnestly, "only we can't tell Father or Mother. You said so yourself."

"We asked them if there were any valuables in the cottage," Carlyle told him, "but Father said only a couple of rare books."

Tee-Bo shook his head stubbornly and started back for his post on the porch. "Bony-Leg wants something in here, and I aim to keep him from getting it. Now, you two go back to the beach. *Somebody* has to have a vacation."

"We'll go down with you when Mother and Father come back," the children promised, anxious to leave before the prowler came back.

"Never mind." Tee-Bo gave them a look that plainly said, "Don't bother about *me*. I'm only a dog. *Anything's* good enough for *me*."

They kept their word, and as soon as their parents returned, browned and hungry, to shower and listen to records and prepare dinner, the three went down to the beach. Here Tee-Bo had an hour of delirious joy, fetching sticks and playing hide-and-seek around the umbrella of a man who wanted to sleep. When the man picked up his belongings and marched away in resigned desperation, Tee-Bo decided he'd had enough.

"Let's go home," he told the children. "I've had my vacation for the day."

The children were tired, too. Dusk was settling over the mountains, and as they neared the cottage, they could see their parents on the porch. There was a third chair occupied, too, and at the sight of this, Tee-Bo stopped in his tracks.

"It's him," he growled, his chin whiskers quivering with agitation.

"What?" cried the children together, but the dog cautioned them to be quiet.

"It's him, on the porch. I mean, it's *he*. Oh, you know! It's Bony-Leg!"

"The prowler?" Cam whispered.

"No one else."

"What shall we do?" asked Carlyle.

"You can't bite him now," Cam warned, looking worried.

"Hah!" Tee-Bo let out a snort. "Don't I know it!

Your father told me all about that place they have for dogs who bite! Forevermore, now what'll I do? Suppose he's told them that I bit him."

"He wouldn't dare," Carlyle said. "Then Father would know he'd been prowling."

"Besides"—Cam patted him reassuringly—"Father has a lot of faith in you."

"He only talks like he doesn't," added Carlyle.

"I sometimes think I know Father better than you do," sighed Tee-Bo, looking vexed. "On the other hand—" He stopped, deep in thought. "Well," he said briskly after a moment, "we can't just stand here. This is a very delicate situation, and we'll all have to try to be as natural as possible. I know I'll growl, because I can't help it, and Father will make me lie in the corner." He sighed. "Well, I was going to lie down, anyway."

They proceeded self-consciously toward the porch, a soft growl deepening in the dog's throat. It changed to a sneeze when he tried to suppress it.

"Never mind," Cam whispered, "the prowler will expect you to growl at him!" That thought made Tee-Bo feel ever so much better.

"Time you came home," Mother called. "We were about to go after you. What's the matter, Tee-Bo?"

"We'd like you to meet our children," Father said. "Our son, Cameron, and—what's the matter, boy?—and our daughter, Carlyle. Children, this is

Mr. Geyser. He tells us he has a cottage down the way— *Now* what ails that dog?"

It was impossible not to stare. The children said, "How do you do?" politely, Carlyle went to the hammock, and Cam took his favorite place on the porch steps.

"You young people look as if you've been having a fine vacation," Mr. Geyser said jovially, keeping one eye on Tee-Bo as he talked. He had the thinnest lips the children had ever seen. He hardly opened them to talk. "What's your little dog's name? He . . . he must be quite a pet."

"His name is Tee-Bo," said Father, "but it will be mud if he doesn't soon quiet down. Tee-Bo, go to your corner!"

"Whatever ails him?" asked Mother. "He doesn't growl at visitors."

"Oh, sometimes he does," Cam said quickly. "I remember once he growled at the milkman—"

"And the postman," Carlyle said, swinging wildly in the hammock, "and once at a friend of yours, Father, when you weren't home."

"Well, I never knew anything about it," said Father, "and you stay there!" he added to Tee-Bo, who had gone meekly to his corner and was now lying there, chin on paws and eyes narrowed, taking in every detail.

"It was kind of you to stop by, Mr. Geyser," said

Mother. "Carlyle! Watch out! You're going clear over the porch! Can I give you another cup of coffee, Mr. Geyser?"

"Just a warm-up, just a warm-up." Mr. Geyser smiled, barely showing a row of teeth.

"It's a shame your mother lost her ring when she had the cottage last summer," Mother said. "You know, it could still be around somewhere."

"You say you looked everywhere? That is, she did, your mother?" Father asked politely.

Mr. Geyser threw his hands out in a gesture, then stared at his nails. "Mother is—well—pretty old now, and, of course, she might have overlooked it. That's why I came back. She feels so bad about losing it that I said I would try to find it. I told her, 'Mother, if it's there, I'll find it!' "

"Dog or no dog?" said Tee-Bo, lifting one eyebrow.

"Well, we'll certainly look," Father declared, nodding gravely but not moving.

"Hah! If he could find a firecracker in a Chinese market—" began Tee-Bo. The children giggled and then stopped and stared.

"Father, you're wearing your sneakers!" Carlyle said.

"So it appears."

"They were in the closet," Mother added.

"They were there when I got home. They were

not there yesterday or the day before."

"So you say," Mother teased.

Tee-Bo snickered. "And he's so right."

"Good boy, Tee-Bo," said Cam.

"My good deed for the day," the dog replied. "I think Father's learned his lesson. Now, keep your eyes peeled and watch that Geyser character. I'm checkmated and don't dare move." He threw, in the direction of their visitor, a look that was so sinister and so full of hidden meaning that Mother, who happened just then to glance that way, was startled.

"Why, look at Tee-Bo!" she exclaimed. "I do believe he's sneering!"

"He probably has a . . . a toothache," Cam said quickly.

Tee-Bo snorted loudly. "Toothache! Well might I have! But we know someone who has a leg ache, and he's not too far off, either!"

Mr. Geyser, at this point, seemed to feel uncomfortable, although he had the best chair. "I should be going, I suppose. But I must thank you folks for the hospitality. You're really . . . great." He chewed his lip and seemed to think about that last word for a moment. "Really great," he repeated, the word apparently having passed the test. "I suppose you'll be going to the beach tomorrow, all of you."

"Every day!" Father said genially.

"We can't keep the children away," said Mother. They had risen to say good-bye.

"All of you, heh-heh." Mr. Geyser had a slow chuckle. "And your—ah—little dog, too?"

"If he behaves himself," said Father.

"Well, I'll be down there myself tomorrow. Ought to get a little sun while I have a chance. Heh-heh."

"You know you're welcome to look around, if you like, but if your mother's ring hasn't been found by now, I wouldn't hope too much." Father was standing first on one foot and then on the other, as he always did when he was starving at dinner time and couldn't bellow because they had company.

"Oh, no! Not at all!" Mr. Geyser protested. "Wouldn't intrude; not at all! Just—you know— don't look for it. Wouldn't trouble you for worlds. See you tomorrow. See you tomorrow at the beach."

"What a thin man," Mother said, when he had gone.

"So fond of his mother," said Father. "I'm hungry." He opened his mouth to bellow.

"Quick!" hissed Tee-Bo. "Ask him about the ring, before he starts caterwauling!"

"Father, did Mr. Geyser's mother really lose a ring? In our cottage?" Cam tumbled the words out all in one breath.

Father looked thoughtful. "If it were a biological possibility for anyone to come into this world without a mother, I would name our recent visitor as a number one prospect."

"Good!" Tee-Bo crowed. "He doesn't believe Bony-Leg!"

"Why, I think he's very nice," Mother protested. "And look at all the trouble he is going to, just to find her ring, which was only a keepsake, he said, and not very valuable at all."

"My dear," Father replied, tweaking her ear ever so gently, "you are a fathomless judge of character, I am a scoundrel, and Mr. Geyser is an unspotted saint. Now—let us dine."

"I couldn't have said it better myself," Tee-Bo declared, following the others into the kitchen.

"I don't care," Mother replied, laying out the dishes. "I still think he is a very pleasant man."

4
A New Friend

The next day it was hot so early that Mother decided they should spend all day at the beach. Tee-Bo went with them.

"But I'm coming right back," he told the children, "to guard the cottage." The children thought it odd that their visitor hadn't mentioned that he'd been there before and that their dog had bitten him, but Tee-Bo said *he* was undeceived.

"Prowlers aren't given to bragging about affairs like that, mark my words," he told them as they lagged behind. "Did you really expect him to say, 'Look; see what your dog did to me when I tried to break in while you were away'?"

"But Mother likes him," Carlyle protested.

"Your mother loves the whole world," Tee-Bo said firmly. "That's why we have to protect her."

To their surprise, when they reached the beach, there sat Mr. Geyser, wearing a pair of magenta swim trunks that called special attention to his long, white legs and gaunt, pale torso. He smiled and waved when he saw them.

"He's an albino," said Tee-Bo, staring unbelievingly at the man.

"Where did you learn about albinos?" asked Cam.

"I'm the dog of a college professor," Tee-Bo reminded him. "Shouldn't that make a difference?"

While the children helped their parents spread out the blanket and beach chairs, Mr. Geyser plodded over to say good morning.

"I see you brought your little dog," he commented, managing to keep one or two of them between him and Tee-Bo.

Tee-Bo bristled a little and said with a growl, "Just take a look at that leg!"

Midway up his calf, Mr. Geyser wore a neat bandage with iodine showing through.

"Iodine indeed!" the dog went on. "I'm the one that needed the disinfectant!"

Meanwhile, Father had accidentally knocked the umbrella pole against their guest. He was grumpy, anyway, because Mother had invited Mr. Geyser to sit down and have a lemonade, and that meant he would have to share part of the blanket with him.

"I beg your pardon," said Father. "I hope I haven't hurt your injured leg. Whatever did you do to it?"

"I did it! It was me!" Tee-Bo's sides rippled, meaning that he was laughing.

Mr. Geyser, trying to keep out of the way while holding his paper cup of lemonade so it wouldn't spill, ducked suddenly and got poked again by the umbrella—this time, right in the middle of his forehead.

"Excuse me! It was really nothing, my leg," he said. "Stepped on a branch in the dark—you know."

"Perhaps you had better sit down," Mother suggested. "We should have warned you that we all lie low until Father gets the umbrella up."

Somehow the umbrella was set up without further injuries, and the children raced off for the river, just a few yards away. Tee-Bo stayed near Mother's edge of the blanket, having dug a hole with his nose where the sand was cool, eyes closed, apparently fast asleep.

"Mr. Geyser," said Mother, reaching for the jug, "will you have more lemonade?"

"Oh, call me Francis, do," begged Mr. Geyser,

almost showing a whole tooth in a smile.

At this, Tee-Bo's head came up with a violent jerk, accompanied by a snort of such force that a good quantity of wet sand remaining on top of his nose made him sneeze and send sand flying in all directions—but principally onto Mr. Geyser.

"Oh, Tee-Bo!" said Mother, covering the open jug with her hand.

"My, oh, my!" Mr. Geyser said, very slowly, as though unfamiliar with the phrase, and began brushing himself off.

"Tee-Bo, out! Go!" Father's tone and his pointing finger were uncompromising. Tee-Bo backed several feet away and stared at the others, his whiskered face the picture of mortification.

"Don't just stand there and *blush*," said Father grimly. "Just *go*. Get out of my sight. I ought to send you back to the cottage, you bouncing, flea-ridden virus!"

"Oh, no!" protested Geyser quickly. "By all means, let him stay. Uh—dogs will be dogs, they say. Heh-heh."

Tee-Bo looked at Mother. Whatever she decided would be final.

"Go on, Tee-Bo, take a run. Good boy," said Mother.

"Father oughtn't to talk to me that way," Tee-Bo muttered, "particularly before strangers."

"You've hurt his feelings," Mother said. "Dear, you know how sensitive he is."

Tee-Bo walked off, looking behind once or twice to see if they were going to call him back, but they just began talking to one another, so he kept on going, chin whiskers trembling as he complained to himself.

"Francis indeed! I'll Francis *him!*" He stalked off down the beach, winding past sunbathers, beach umbrellas, inner tubes, beach sandals, and even a delicious morsel of hot dog, which at any other time he would have gobbled up in passing.

"Father is an ungrateful beast!" he finally declared quite loudly. This caused him to feel better, and he trotted away over the sand, until he heard an unknown voice calling to him.

"Hello, boy. Come here! Come here!"

On the beach, a little way off, sat a young man in swim trunks, burned as brown as a coconut, with bright blue eyes sparkling in a face full of good humor and friendliness.

"Come on, boy, come on!" the young man was saying, snapping his fingers at him.

"Why should I?" asked Tee-Bo, stopping. "You might be a dognapper."

"Here, want to fetch? Go fetch!" He threw a stick into the river, where it floated lazily with the current. "Go on, fetch it! Fetch, boy!"

"I don't see why I should," said Tee-Bo. "Go get it yourself if you want it."

"So, you won't fetch for me." The young man seemed pleased. "I know you understand. I've seen you with the children, but you don't jump at everybody's command, do you? Stout fellow. Commendable trait."

Tee-Bo stood and stared for nearly an entire minute. There was something appealing about the stranger. His skin was smooth and healthy-looking, his fair hair was rumpled by the breeze, and his grin was wide, showing white teeth. Tee-Bo decided he looked much like Cameron, in a few years' time, and like Father, before he became a history professor. The young man was very good-looking, and his voice was reassuring.

"But Father is good-looking, too," Tee-Bo added quickly, for he was loyal to the core and rarely held a grudge.

"I'm somewhat annoyed with my master," he said to the young man, "and if you knew what I know, you'd see I have reason to be."

"What's wrong, fella? Come on, let's be friends." The young man surveyed him with a look of such good humor that Tee-Bo's peevishness melted away. He lay down on the sand, chin on his paws, getting a closer look at the stranger.

"I wish you spoke my language," Tee-Bo told

him. "You and I would have a long talk."

"What's on your mind, fella?" asked the young man. "Problems?"

Tee-Bo groaned. "You should meet Francis," he said, "and you wouldn't ask!"

At this moment, he heard the children calling and whistling to him from far down the beach, and when he wouldn't answer, they raced up to see why, arriving in a shower of sand, with water still running off their suits.

"Why didn't you come when we called?" Cam asked, dropping down beside him.

"Please—you're cold and wet," Tee-Bo said politely. "I heard you call, but I wanted you to come here."

"Why?" Cam asked, then said, "Oh," awkwardly, knowing how it would sound to someone who could not understand Tee-Bo. "This is our dog, Tee-Bo," he said to the young man.

"I know." He smiled, and Tee-Bo could see that the children liked him, too.

"I'm Carlyle, and this is my brother, Cameron. He's a year older than I am," said Carlyle, who was never bashful before strangers. "We're Dr. McRae's children. Our parents are over there under that beach umbrella—the white one with the blue fringe."

"I know," the young man said again.

"I didn't tell him a thing," Tee-Bo said, "but he's sharp."

"My name is Larry Blade," the young man went on, "but my friends call me Racer. I hope we can be friends."

"Tee-Bo likes you," Cam said.

"Tee-Bo is a good dog," Racer said. "He's very intelligent. I wish I had a dog. I wish I had a friend."

"Are you here all alone?" asked Carlyle, in her mother's tones of solicitude.

"All alone."

"Don't you have any family?"

"Carlyle!" Her brother scowled at her. "You're not supposed to ask people things like that!"

"Oh, I'm glad to have someone to talk with, really," the young man said. "You see, just between the three of us—"

"Leave me out," interrupted Tee-Bo. "Everybody else does."

"Just between the *four* of us," the young man went on, just as if he had heard, "I do have a family, but it's awfully new. I have a . . . a brand-new . . . wife, but"—here he stopped smiling, and his blue eyes looked sad—"we had a sort of quarrel, and she wouldn't come with me on my . . . on our vacation."

"Then why didn't you stay with her?" asked Carlyle.

Racer looked rather astonished but went on to explain. "Because I'd already engaged the cottage, and I hoped she would give in and follow me if I came, anyway." He sighed. "But I'm still waiting, and it's very lonely."

"You can come over to *our* cottage," Carlyle said decisively, giving her head a vigorous nod. "Mother would be pleased, and Father would tell you all about the Mongolians. He's writing a book with his friend Arthur—"

"It's a dictionary," Cam put in.

"A dictionary," Carlyle continued, "because there aren't any English-Mongolian dictionaries in the whole world, and Father doesn't have anybody to talk to about it up here. He's already told us a hundred times."

The young man looked first thoughtful and then sadder than ever. "Yes, that would be very nice," he agreed, "but I would be intruding, and that isn't polite, you know."

Cam, who was doing a headstand nearby, got to his feet quickly. "Father would be glad to have company. He doesn't like Mr. Geyser very much."

Tee-Bo sniffed loudly. "You mean *Francis*. Did you know his first name is *Francis*?"

The children exchanged delighted glances but tried not to giggle, knowing that the stranger could not hear the dog.

"Mr. Blade," Carlyle said, "is it all right if we tell anyone about you and your wife having a quarrel? I mean Mother and Father. They'd be sorry for you."

Cam nodded. "They might help you. Father is always helping students with their problems."

"Only he says it's Mother's pies that do it," Carlyle added.

"I'm sure it will be perfectly all right to tell them all about me," said Mr. Blade solemnly, "but don't let them think I would impose or anything, because I wouldn't for the world—though I'm terribly interested in the Mongolians."

"You are?" the children exclaimed.

"I really am."

"We'd better go tell Father," Carlyle said. "He won't believe it, though. Good-bye, Mr. Blade, and don't worry about a thing."

"I'll see you tomorrow or the day after," Mr. Blade called after them as they ran off.

Tee-Bo stayed behind for a moment, his head to one side, staring at the young man as though puzzled.

"You *are* a strange one," he said finally. "I didn't quite swallow that story about your wife, but the one about the Mongolians—never in a month of Sundays!"

"Tee-Bo," said Mr. Blade, "I have an idea that,

if dogs could talk, you could give me an earful. You're a likable chap, but I don't think you quite trust me."

"You're a likable chap, too," Tee-Bo said, "and you're absolutely right. But, forevermore, I'm not sure that I don't like you, anyway."

"Better be off, boy; they're paging you," advised Mr. Blade.

As Tee-Bo left, he noticed that the young man was smiling again, looking as happy as a lark and seeming to have forgotten he'd ever had a quarrel *or* a wife.

5
The Robber Again

The children were disgruntled to find Mr. Geyser
still there, sipping lemonade, with Father expound-
ing, as usual, on his favorite topic: the Mongolians.

"And these laws," he was saying, "laid down by
Genghis Khan were so moderate, so just, so *ad-
vanced* that the Mongols abided by them for two
hundred years after his death, in absolute peace and
harmony."

"Is that a fact?" Mr. Geyser, who had been sub-
jected to a forty-five-minute discourse on the vir-
tues of the great khan, wore the expression of a man
who has been invitcd to ride over Niagara Falls—

without benefit of even a barrel.

"Mother—" Carlyle began.

"Now, you take our western writers," Father went on, steaming into his favorite topic with all the finesse of a runaway locomotive, "one in particular, whose name I won't mention, but I'm sure you know whom I mean—"

"Look at Francis!" Tee-Bo snickered. "This is killing him!"

"Mother," said Carlyle, "we met—"

"They've tried to make us swallow, hook, line, and sinker," continued Father, beginning really to warm up now, "stories of the savagery and cruelty of the Mongol peoples, until our knowledge of them, our impression of this truly great race, is as far from the truth as we are from—"

"The River Roknobad," said Tee-Bo.

"Tee-Bo!" said Carlyle.

"Well," said Tee-Bo, "he always says that."

". . . the River Roknobad!" Father finished emphatically, nodding his head.

"Eh? Where's that?" Mr. Geyser looked startled.

"Tell her now," said Tee-Bo, "but hurry!"

Carlyle drew a deep breath. "Mother, we met a friend, and he had a quarrel with his wife, and she's a new one, and he said we could tell you, and why don't you give him some of your pie?"

"He's lonely and doesn't have any company,

only problems," Cam offered, "and he's nice, too."

Since no one said a word, Carlyle continued, "Well, Father always says your pies set the world to rights, don't you, Father?"

Father nodded vigorously. "I do indeed!"

"I'm flattered," said Mother, smiling. "Did you learn your friend's name?"

"His name's Larry Blade," said Cameron.

"His friends call him Racer, and he's right over there," said Carlyle, pointing.

Mr. Geyser now spoke up, his voice suddenly sounding hard. "I'd be mighty careful who I let my kids take up with." Then, having second thoughts, he added, "Of course, here at a summer resort, we're all sort of—" he waved a hand and smiled feebly— "we're all sort of familiar, you might say. . . ."

"Too familiar," Tee-Bo said loudly, "in the case of you-know-who."

"Our children," Father stated, as though issuing an ultimatum at the U.N., "pick up acquaintances like noses do freckles and dogs fleas."

"Hey-ho!" cried Tee-Bo, with a toss of his head. "Compliments again!"

"It's a phenomenon of nature," Father went on. "They attract people as if we were rich."

"They wear little magnets inside their clothes," Mother agreed.

"Tell your friend," Father said, "Mr. . . . ah . . .

Mr.— What was the name you said?"

"Blade," said the children.

"Blade," he continued, "that we hold open house twenty-four hours a day, but it's purely involuntary, and Pie Day is a week away—continuously."

"How unfriendly!" Mother remarked. "And you were voted one of the ten most popular teachers last year."

"No, I was voted one of the ten most intelligent," retorted Father, "and that does not make me friendly—only conceited. But rather than have you think me misanthropic, my dear, I will make you a sign to hang on our door: FRESH PIE AND SYMPATHY SERVED HERE EVERY DAY ON THE HOUR. ARSENIC OPTIONAL BUT STRONGLY URGED BY THE HOST."

"Look at that fellow standing over by those trees," Tee-Bo said in a low voice to Cam, who was close. "He just signaled; watch him."

A man in a dark suit, a dark hat, and dark shoes stood in the shade some distance away. As Cam looked, the stranger jerked his head down, as if nodding, then turned and walked swiftly away.

"I've never seen him before," said Tee-Bo, "not that I was missing anything. One of dear Francis's friends, I guess."

Mr. Geyser was rising, shaking sand from his beach towel, and sliding his long, white feet into slippers.

"It's been a real enjoyment, folks," he said, casting a quick look at Tee-Bo and then barely grinning at the children's parents. "We should do this often. I feel I must go, however."

"Well, since you got your signal and all," remarked the dog, "but we hate to see you go. It leaves such a gap."

"Now, there goes a fine, upstanding chap," declared Mother as their guest plodded over the sand toward the trees.

"What?" said Father.

"I was only saying it for you," Mother replied, beginning to pick up the things. "Any chap who will listen for an hour straight to a discourse on the Mongols is, by default, a fine, upstanding chap."

"Are you intimating that I bored him?" Father queried.

"No, indeed!" asserted Mother. "Such an intimation is unnecessary. You already know it."

"I was hoping he would be bored enough to leave," Father said disconsolately. "Jove!" He began to laugh. "I was rather ponderous, wasn't I?"

"Beautifully," agreed Mother, "but let's swim. The last one in is a plum-faced platypus."

The children raced over the sand behind their parents.

"Where's Tee-Bo?" Cam asked, coming up after a headlong dive into the water.

"He must have gone after you-know-who!" Carlyle said. "Do you think we should follow him?"

"It's too hot," Cam said. "I'm just going to stay in the water and pretend I'm a frog."

Carlyle scowled. "Well, I can't pretend that."

"Why not?"

"I was the last one in. I'm a plum-faced platypus, so I can't be a frog."

"Tell you what," Cam decided. "When we finish swimming, let's go see Mr. Blade and talk to him some more."

But when they looked for him a little later, the spot he had occupied was empty, and they could not find him anywhere on the beach.

At day's end, they walked up the stairs toward the cottage, sunburned, windburned, and sleepy. Father, for once, had got off the subject of the Mongols and was telling how a heavenly body made its first appearance, as a comet, between the fifteenth and eighth centuries B.C. and how, in coming too close to Earth's orbit, it's gravitational pull had caused strange disturbances on Earth. The children were fascinated. This was a tale they never wearied of hearing, for, as Father told it, it was almost as exciting as being there.

Mother went in ahead to turn on the lamps, while Father hung beach towels and suits on the line. The children, having hung up their things, sat in the hammock, yawning and calling for Tee-Bo, who was absent.

After a few moments, Mother opened the screen door and slowly walked out onto the porch. She just stood there, saying nothing.

"What's the matter?" asked Father quickly, looking up at her.

"I'm not quite sure," said Mother, "but I had the strangest sensation when I first went in. Come in and see if you notice it. Don't touch anything. Just look."

"Stay here, small fry," Father said. He was up the stairs in two bounds.

The children could hear their parents moving about in the house, going from room to room and exclaiming occasionally. When they came back to the front room, off the porch, Mother could be heard quite distinctly, saying, "I can't say exactly what it is, but it's as though everything had been picked up and then put down just a little differently from the way it was before."

"Could be your imagination, my dear," Father said lightly. "You probably tidied up this morning while conjugating a Greek verb."

"The prowler!" Cam whispered. "He's been here again!"

"But Mr. Geyser is the prowler," Carlyle said, "and he was at the beach almost all day."

Cam shook his head knowingly. "We'll ask Tee-Bo. He'll know."

But when it came time to feed Tee-Bo after supper, he was not there.

"Where *is* that dog?" Father grumbled. He was in a temper, anyway, about something and kept stalking about the rooms, looking at the bookcase, and shaking his head with a puzzled air.

He went out on the porch and called, "Hey, *Teeee-Booooooooooooo!*" For a mild, soft-spoken man, Father could muster up a bellow that caused rocks to bounce, and when he called children or dogs that way, they generally responded without stopping to weigh matters.

"Hey, *Teeeeee-Boooooooooooo!*" he called again, but still the dog failed to appear. "I suspect he'll come scratching at the door about three in the morning, and *I'll* be the only one to hear him!"

Father sighed and double-checked the kitchen door.

"You're sure you didn't straighten up the house this morning?" he said to Mother, before turning out the light.

"I made sandwiches and lemonade and did the breakfast dishes. Oh, and the beds. And that's all. Why?"

"It's my books," explained Father. "Someone's put Ibn Batuta right next to Immanuel Kant—

right smack-dab against it!"

"Well, my dear—" Mother yawned—"it was bound to happen someday."

Father stared at her as though she had suddenly taken leave of her senses. "The world's greatest traveler," he said slowly, "snuggled, positively snuggled, up against the works of a man who never went farther than three miles from the place where he was born? It's pure bad taste. It's inconceivable. Not even the children would do that; certainly, my dear, not you!"

"Never," said Mother, "*not ever*. Not—" yawn— "since the time I put Montaigne next to Goethe and you almost skinned me alive—dear."

"What a horrid, repulsive impossibility!"

"Oh, but you didn't do it!"

"No," Father explained, "I mean putting a prince of a fellow like Montaigne next to that German rogue."

At three o'clock in the morning, Tee-Bo came home and, finding the door locked, sat on the step, scratching with his paw on the screen and uttering soft little whines.

"If I bark," he said to himself, "the children will wake up, but if I just scratch, Father will be the only one to hear me."

It was not long before the bed gave a great creak and a low-toned bellow was heard issuing from the

bedroom. Tee-Bo scratched louder. Next came a thud as two bare feet hit the floor, followed by the shuffling of slippers moving toward the back door.

"Come in, you monster"—Father pushed the screen open—"and if you wake the children, I'll skin you alive every day for a year."

Tee-Bo slipped in, making himself as thin as possible.

"That would be quite an achievement," he murmured as he passed Father, "but if you knew what I know, it wouldn't be me as got skinned, no, sir!"

The next day, Mother decided that she and Father would stay at the cottage instead of going down to the river. Father had research to do, and she wanted to wash her hair and some clothes. Father lectured Tee-Bo for one minute and the children for half a minute about getting up in "the dead of night" to let in worthless beasts who never even bothered to thank a person, but midway in his tirade, he forgot why he was annoyed and began telling them about Ibn Batuta, the great Arabian traveler, who had once witnessed a Mongol chieftain, Bashti, clad in full armor, jumping over the back of a standing camel *nine times*.

"That man's attention span is shorter than his temper," remarked Tee-Bo, with a toss of his head. "What has this fellow, I Been Batuti, got to do with me staying out late?"

"Tee-Bo—" Carlyle snickered—"it's Ibn Batuta, not— What was it you called him?"

"Children," said Mother, "Father is studying— or supposed to be—and it isn't snowing, so out, out!"

"I wish I could skate," sighed Carlyle.

"Skate!" Mother laughed. "Forevermore, you can skate all winter, so go out now and play in the dust and sand. Your chores are done, I presume."

"Mine are!" the children chorused as they fled the house, Tee-Bo at their heels.

"Why does Father always work on his vacation?" Cam said, chinning himself on the limb of a tree.

"Work!" sniffed Tee-Bo. "He's not working! He's reading. That man would rather read than . . . than be a hero!"

"A hero? What do you mean, Tee-Bo?" asked Carlyle, getting down on her knees and ruffling his fur. Tee-Bo walked away and sat down in the shade, his expression something less than happy.

"I'm an educated dog. I hope I mean 'hero' when I say it."

Cam, now hanging by his knees, stared at him thoughtfully. "You *are* an educated dog, aren't you?"

"I most certainly am. How could I help it, in this family? I'm also slightly balmy in the crumpet— same reason."

"I don't see why you're so cross," Carlyle said. "I didn't mean to hurt your feelings. How could Father be a hero?"

"By getting his nose out of a book for once and using it for something useful!" snapped the dog.

"Tee-Bo," Cam went on, still thoughtfully, "if you belonged to a Chinese family, you'd speak Chinese, wouldn't you?"

"Fluently, of course."

The children were silent a moment, picturing Tee-Bo conversing eloquently in Chinese, replete with Mandarin costume and queue. Cam began to giggle but stopped, seeing the expression on the dog's face. Carlyle moved close to Tee-Bo and hugged him.

"Oh, Tee-Bo, we love you just the way you are! We're glad you belong to us! But why are you so grumbly today?"

"I was up late last night," Tee-Bo answered, looking self-conscious and somewhat repentant, "and I'm upset about something. I can't talk about it. It's nothing you did."

"That reminds me!" Cam said. "We were going to ask you something important, remember, Carly?"

"Oh!" His sister's eyes grew big. "About the prowler!"

"And what about him?" asked Tee-Bo, looking cross again. They told him what had happened and that their parents believed someone had ransacked the cottage and then carefully put everything back, only some things were put in the wrong place.

Tee-Bo listened carefully. "Humph! Pretty persnickety prowler," he growled sarcastically.

Carlyle ignored Tee-Bo. "We know that the prowler, Mr. Geyser, was at the beach yesterday. He couldn't have done it," Carlyle finished.

"All crooks have accomplices," her brother retorted. "Someone else could have done it while Mr. Geyser made sure we were away. That's probably why he hung around!"

Tee-Bo was staring worriedly at the boy. Now he uttered a great snort of derision. "Spare yourself the amateur sleuthing," he said, acting as if it all bored him. "You'll just get into trouble."

Cam looked at him in surprise. "I thought you wanted to solve this mystery."

"I think you should drop the whole thing." Tee-Bo's tones were so final that both children stared.

"You're covering up something, aren't you, boy?" asked Cam. "You must have found out something you won't tell us."

"For pity's sake," Tee-Bo cried out, just the way Mother would have, "let us drop the discussion right here! I have a problem to work out, and that's the long and the short of it."

"Maybe you're coming down with something," Carlyle suggested. "Let me feel your nose."

"Go and feel Father's nose!" retorted Tee-Bo rudely. "He's the one who should be worried, not *me*. I'm just a dog." He looked so mournful that the children did not have the heart to reply.

"You really must forgive me," he said with a gulp. "I have to go off and think things over. I need some time alone."

6
Behind the Bookcase

It wasn't much fun without Tee-Bo, but Carlyle found a book she hadn't read for a long time, and Cam made a quail call from a twig and a leaf of the bay tree, just the way a hunter friend of Father's had taught him. The day grew warmer and drowsier, and before they knew it, afternoon had already arrived.

"This is the best book I've ever read," Carlyle said as she finished the last page.

"You always say that," her brother replied. "How come you can read so fast? It took me two days. Did you skip?"

"Only the part about the history of the man's family— " She broke off suddenly. "Someone's coming up the road."

Cam jumped up. "It's Mr. Blade!"

The children ran to greet him.

"This is a charming cottage," said their visitor. He was looking mournful again.

"Come in," Carlyle invited him. "Mother and Father are both home. Did your wife get here yet?"

"No, not yet." He sighed and came through the gate.

"You could phone her," said Carlyle. "I was thinking about that."

"Carly, for Pete's sake—" her brother began, but their visitor interrupted gently.

"No, no, she's right. But I did. I phoned her six times yesterday. She's just . . . thinking it over, you know."

"I know." Carlyle nodded. "Like Father and Mother."

"Where's the dog? Where's Tee-Bo?" asked Mr. Blade, looking around.

"Oh, he's gone somewhere. He has a problem," Cam said.

"Tee-Bo, too? Hmm. Oh, I do hope your parents won't think I'm intruding. Perhaps they're busy."

"Oh, they never do anything," Cam said cheerfully. "Come on in."

They were walking across the yard, when Father came out onto the porch.

"Father, this is the Mr. Blade we were telling you about," Carlyle explained.

Father came down the steps, extending his hand. "Delighted to have you call," he said. "Our name is McRae, in case the children forgot to mention it."

"I know, Dr. McRae," the young man said.

"Well, it's just teatime. Do come in."

"Oh, I was just passing by," the other protested.

"Glad you did." Father talked as if it were pre-arranged, which was one of the nice things he did to put people at ease. "Come along, now. Mother's probably set the cups out already."

But when he had introduced their guest and they were seated at the table, Father began to bellow softly.

"What! No pie!"

"No pie," Mother told him cheerfully. "Tea and cookies today."

"Can't settle problems without pie," Father declared, still mildly outraged.

"Who has a problem?" asked Mother, as if it were a new word.

"Tee-Bo!" both children cried at once.

Mother frowned. "Is he sick?"

"No, just cross and grumbly."

"He should complain," said Father. "He doesn't

have to get up at three in the morning to let *me* in!"

"Lucky for you, too!" said Mother, her eyes laughing at Father over the rim of her cup.

"These cookies are absolutely delicious," Mr. Blade said, reaching for a third one.

"I'd be glad to give the recipe to your wife, if she wants it."

"Mother, we *told* you—" Carlyle began.

"I believe," Mother interrupted gently, "I was addressing Mr. Blade."

"Oops, scuse me." Carlyle reached for a cookie to hide her embarrassment.

"It's perfectly all right," Mr. Blade said, looking earnestly mournful once more. "I'm glad the children told you about me and my wife. It explains why I'm taking my vacation alone. But if my . . . my wife joins me here—and I'm sure she will; at least, I'm hoping she will—then she would certainly like to have the recipe." He sighed and cast a woebegone look about the room. "You have a nice place here—and so many books."

Father raised his eyebrows. "Many? Why, we just brought a few."

"I notice there isn't any library in town," their guest remarked.

"There's one at Santa Rosa, but I don't know how good it is," said Father. "We'll be going there soon, I'm sure, before my daughter runs out of books. She would read from sunup to sundown if it were not for an occasional diversion."

"Like sleeping and eating," Mother added.

"Libraries aren't what they used to be," Father sighed. "In the good old days, librarians not only read books but could also discuss them with a fair amount of intelligence. But then, you're too young to know much about the good old days, I guess."

"I'm older than I look," Mr. Blade said modestly. "Some of these books appear to be quite valuable, if I'm not mistaken."

"Oh, they are!" declared Father, jumping up and going to the shelves. "This one. . . ." He selected a book and began a discourse on it. He was on the verge of forgetting his guest entirely.

"Ah . . . well . . ." interrupted Mr. Blade, with surprising boldness, "do you think it . . . uh . . . well . . . safe to leave such books unguarded? You know, there might be— But I don't suppose there are—"

"Prowlers?" Cam and Carlyle supplied the word in unison.

"Odd you should mention that," Father murmured, coming abruptly out of his reverie. He was about to continue, but he just opened his mouth instead and looked at Mother helplessly.

"Children," Mother said, coming to the rescue, "you've finished your tea, so we'll excuse you. Take some cookies with you, and don't go too far."

"I didn't want to talk about it in front of them," Father explained when the children had gone, "but we believe someone broke into our cottage yester-day while we were at the beach."

"What makes you think so?" asked Mr. Blade. "Was something taken?"

"Nothing!" the two answered together, and Mother went on to explain. "It's just that we're sure someone was here. I came into the house first, and I had the strangest sensation—the feeling you get when things have been moved and a familiar room just isn't familiar anymore."

"How do you mean that?" Mr. Blade asked, his voice not at all slow or mournful now.

Mother shrugged. "Things were off-key. It was just as if the place had been thoroughly searched and then everything carefully put back."

"But put back wrong," Father declared. "For instance, my books—"

"And the towels in the linen closet."

"And my razor."

"And some boxes I keep on the bathroom shelves. I always keep them on the right side, but they were all piled neatly on the left. It's ridiculous!"

"Nothing was missing?"

"Nothing," said Father, "unless they took something we didn't know was here."

A strange look shot across Mr. Blade's warm blue eyes, and they became cold and veiled. Then it was gone, and his eyes were mournful and friendly again.

"Well," he said cheerfully, "in that case, you'll never miss it, will you?"

"It puzzles me," Mother said, "and I don't like it one bit. But since we'll be here only one more week, and since nothing of ours was taken, we've decided not to worry about it."

"There's probably nothing to worry about," Mr. Blade said drowsily.

"Have another cookie," said Father. "At your age, I would have finished off the plate by this time."

"Oh, I'm older than I look," Mr. Blade said once more, as if apologizing for it.

"You're certainly welcome to borrow any of these," Father said, going to the bookcase as their guest was preparing to leave. "I've got books on travel, biographies, journals. . . ." He raised his hand and pushed on a book that protruded and, when it would not budge, gave it a vigorous little shove. Suddenly, to their astonishment, a portion of the shelf gave way, opening like a cupboard door, and the book fell back out of sight. At the same moment, Carlyle and Cam came in, their eyes popping wide open as they saw what was happening.

"Oho!" cried Father. "What's this?" He reached

his hand in, felt around, and brought the book back. Mr. Blade, who had leaped to his feet as silently as a cat, was at his side. He put out his hand and pushed, and the compartment opened. Without a word, he moved his hand rapidly around the inside, covering every inch, and then withdrew it.

"I never knew *that* was there," said Father, too amazed at finding the secret place to be amazed at Mr. Blade's actions.

"What is it, Father," Cam asked, "a real secret compartment?"

"It *was* secret, at least from me," Father said. "Did you know this was here?" he asked Mother. Then an odd expression crossed both their faces as they stared at each other.

"I noticed, too," she said. "It's right behind Ibn Batuta."

"What's that?" asked Blade quickly.

"It's not a that," Father replied. "It's a book."

That night Tee-Bo stayed away again. He did not come home at three o'clock in the morning, either, but at breakfast time, there he was, snoring peacefully on the porch, where Father almost stepped on him.

"Tee-Bo!" Father bellowed softly, so as not to awaken the other members of his family. "Don't you ever look where I'm going?" Tee-Bo scrambled out of the way as fast as he could and sat down on

the end of the porch, his jaws stretching in a prodigious yawn.

"If I thought you could understand me," Tee-Bo said plaintively as Father went down and up, taking his exercise in the early morning air, "I would call you an ungrateful cad. After all I've done for you, too!"

Father started to go into the house but stopped to look back at the dog, who still eyed him.

"You look terrible," he said, shaking his head. "You ought not to go running around the woods at night. Someone might take a potshot at you."

"Hah!" Tee-Bo snorted. "If you only knew!"

It was not long before the children came out, and Tee-Bo approached them with a warning look in his eye.

"Quick!" he said in low tones. "We've got work to do! Had your breakfast?"

When they said no, he told them to hurry and eat. "Your mother will never let you go anywhere without breakfast," he lamented.

"Where are we going?" the children asked, speaking in low tones, too.

"Never mind. Go eat."

"Will you wait?" they asked.

"Can pigs fly?" he retorted. "No, they can't, but that doesn't mean I won't wait. You know I will!"

But after breakfast there were chores to do, and

then they were set to bathing and dressing, so their parents could take them to an outdoor concert that began at noon in Santa Rosa.

"We can't help it, Tee-Bo," they told him, "but we'll get back as soon as we can."

"That may be too late," he replied, "but far be it from me to interrupt the course of culture. Your parents want you to hear music—so go to the concert. I'll stay here and fight the Indians *and* the cowboys, all by myself."

He would not tell them another word, merely insisting that he would explain everything when they got back.

"Like limburger cheese," Tee-Bo said solemnly, "it'll keep."

7
What Was Hidden in the River

When they returned, it was late afternoon, and Tee-Bo's temper was not at all improved by the delay.

"It's one thing to go to a concert," he complained, "but what were you doing? Learning to play the instruments?"

"We had a hamburger at a drive-in," Cam explained. "Now tell us what happened."

"In an hour it'll be dark," the dog grumbled, "and you shouldn't be out in the woods after dark."

"Are we going to the woods?" asked Carlyle.

"Through the woods to the river—if you can get

permission, now that it's so late."

"I'll ask." Carlyle flew into the house. "We have to be back in an hour," she said, returning a moment later.

"Let's get moving, then," said Tee-Bo.

He led them through the woods to a path that ran beside the river. It was gloomy, chill, and shadowy here, the trees growing tall and forming a thick and leafy roof overhead. Their feet made no sound on the deep carpet of leaves. Tee-Bo began his story the moment they started.

"I said Bony-Leg wanted something in our cottage, remember?" The children nodded. "Well, I was right. He did."

"What was it?" asked Cam as the dog came to a significant silence.

"For goodness' sake," Tee-Bo complained, "let me tell this my own way. We'll get to that later. Besides, I don't know. I just know he wanted *something* out of the cottage, and he got it—whatever it was."

"He got it?" echoed the children in surprise.

"Yep. He got it. The day we were all at the beach."

"Then Mother and Father were right," Carlyle said, her voice excited. "There *was* a prowler, and he was the one who put things back in the wrong place. But why—"

"Wait a minute," Cam interrupted. "If Bony-Leg —I mean Mr. Geyser—was at the beach with us, how could he have searched our cottage?"

"*He* didn't do it, no, sir! It was one of his crooked colleagues. I borrowed that phrase from your father," Tee-Bo said, a bit self-consciously, "and it fits to a T. There's a whole raft of thieves —a whole hive of them—and not too far off. I learned all this the other night when I stayed out so late. I think Bony-Leg is the boss. He gives the orders, anyway, and he has working for him the most fearsome gang I've ever seen. And their names! You wouldn't believe them! There's Scoop—" Tee-Bo paused in the path and nodded, as though counting—"and Nose-Job and Itchy—why, even the Mongolians don't have such crazy names—and, oh, yes, Sniffer. Whew! He's the ugliest one of all!"

"Where did you see them?" Cam asked as they went on. "Where were they?"

"I followed their trail, down this path and across the dam, to the old house on the hill."

"The old haunted house?" Carlyle said, looking about cautiously. "No one has lived there for years!"

"That's where they're staying," Tee-Bo went on in solemn tones, "every last one of them. I went right up and watched through an open window. They were arguing what to do about . . . *it!*"

"What's *it?*" the children asked together.

"A box. It was on the table. They had stolen it from the cottage, and they had to hide it somewhere for a couple of days, until a fellow named Contact came for it. This Contact, whoever he is, was late, and they were all mad at him and mad at each other, and they couldn't decide what to do with the box. Bony-Leg and Scoop almost got into a fight—you know, fisticuffs."

"Tee-Bo," Carlyle asked worriedly, "how much farther are we going?"

They had stopped again. It was very quiet on the river at this hour. The bathers and boaters were at home, putting salve on their sunburn or eating dinner or writing cards. Now it was the fishes', turtles', and crawdads' turn, and they were making the most of it. A soft plopping sound came to their ears.

"What's that?" exclaimed Tee-Bo, startled.

"Only a fish," Cam said, "after a bug."

"I'm a little nervous," said the dog, "understandably so. What's that dark shadow down there?"

"Old Man Hart's boat," Cam said. "It's half-full of water, and the oars are gone. It's been there for a couple of years."

"Well, hurry!" Tee-Bo urged. "We're almost there. And don't talk. Don't even whisper unless you have to. Just follow me."

He slowed down a moment later, sniffing the path from side to side. "I have a keen sense of smell," he explained. Then he came to a dead stop and stood there, listening. "All right, we're here," he told them. "Now, do as I say, and be so quiet you won't even be able to hear yourself."

He went down the bank and through the underbrush to the wet sand at the water's edge, the children at his heels. It was so still, all they could hear was the murmur of the river as it flowed gently by.

"Cam," Tee-Bo said, his voice strained with excitement, "go a little way out on that log and reach down in the water. Don't worry; it'll hold you. You'll find a rope there. Pull it up and get the box. It's tied to the end of the rope."

Cam, his eyes as big as saucers, moved toward the log and began to go slowly along it on his knees. Part of it was on the sand, but a good portion floated on the water, and they could hear the lap-lap of the ripples as the log moved under the boy's weight. It was now so dark under the trees that Cam was only a shadow, his face a white patch in the gloom.

Suddenly there was a soft splashing of water.

"I've found it!" came Cam's hoarse whisper.

"Hurry!" Carlyle whispered, shivering.

"It's weighted down. Just a minute." They could hear him breathing hard as he worked.

"There, I've got it!" he said again and began crawling backward on the log. "Look!" he whispered, when he was standing on the damp sand with them once more. "It's a little chest. It was in a waterproof sack of some sort, but I took it out and let the sack down in the water again. It sure was heavy."

"That's the box!" Tee-Bo said, his whiskers trembling. "Good boy, Cam! Now, let's—"

He stopped, and for a half second there was a terrible silence. The children looked up. Before them loomed the unmoving figure of a man, his arms, legs, and head all shadowy and dark.

"It's Scoop!" cried Tee-Bo, and, with a tremendous leap, he jumped straight at the shadowy figure, a fierce growl gurgling in his throat.

"Run for it!" he cried as he fell back to the ground and leaped again. "I'll fight him off! Run!"

"You run, too, Tee-Bo!" Cam yelled, and he grabbed Carlyle's hand, pulling her along the path with him.

They were running with all their might, when they heard a short, high yelp from Tee-Bo—and then silence.

"Oh, poor Tee-Bo!" cried Carlyle, and, as she turned her head to look back, she caught her foot in a tree root and went sprawling facedown in the leaves.

"Get up!" her brother urged. "I think that man's coming after us!"

Poor Carlyle had the wind knocked out of her, and all she could do was to double over on the path, with leaves and dust clinging to her, and hug her stomach.

"Get up! Get up, Carly," Cam begged. "He's coming!"

"Hide . . . the . . . box!" she panted.

"Where? In the leaves?"

"In the boat. In Old Man Hart's boat. Under the seat. I hid an orange there last year, and it's still there! Hurry!"

Cam leaped to the boat's side and was back on the path in a moment. He grabbed his sister's hand, and they were just running off, when a hand fell heavily on each of them. They were whirled about on the path, and an ugly voice snarled, "One sound outta y'z an' I'll bash y'r heads in!"

8

A Desperate Plight

In the dark, all the children could see was a shadowy figure with a white shirt and, above this, a face almost as white.

"One sound," he repeated, tightening his hold on them, "an' ya'll wish ya hadn't! Git me?"

Neither of the children answered. They were too scared to talk. Scoop pursed his lips in a low whistle. Then he waited. A moment later, another figure came up to them out of the shadows.

"Is it dere?" Scoop said in his harsh voice.

"Nah. Da brats took it, like ya said."

"Awright," Scoop growled, "youse kids listen

good. Ya stoled private propitty. Wha'dja do wit'
it? Come on, come on! Wha'dja do wit' dat box y'z
drug up outta da water, huh? Huh?"

"Ouch!" said Cam, for Scoop was pinching his
arm. "You'd better not pinch me any more. I bruise
very easily, and my parents won't like it."

"Y'r pairnts ain't gonna see y'z no more if we
don't fin' dat box. Where'dja put it? Come on!"

"He threw it into the water," Carlyle said, speaking slowly and distinctly, "as far out as he could.
It sank."

Scoop brought his face down close to Cam's. "Ya
t'rew it inna water, ya dumb kid? Wha'dja do dat
fer?"

"You scared me," Cam said, "so I threw it—into
the middle of the river—and it sank."

"Right here, huh?"

"No. Back there a little way."

"Show me."

He shoved the children ahead of him, and the
four of them went back over the path. When they
were a little distance past the rowboat, Cam said,
"Here."

"Right here?" asked Scoop.

"Yes. By this tree. Right by this tree."

"Itchy," said Scoop, "leave a mark."

"Ya t'ink dem brats is tellin' da trut'?" asked
Itchy uneasily.

"Dey better be," Scoop growled.

"It was right here," Cam said. "I heard it splash when it hit the water."

"Now whadda we do?" Itchy inquired, scratching himself.

"Take da dumb kids back wit' us. Da boss is gotta know."

"He'll boil."

"We'll *fry*, if we don't move fast. Git movin'!"

"Did you hurt our dog?" Carlyle asked, sounding as if she had something in her throat.

Scoop started to speak, then changed his mind and said, instead, "Naw. He up an' beat it. High-tailed fer home."

Both children knew that Tee-Bo would never do that, but neither said a word. If Tee-Bo was hurt, neither Scoop nor Itchy would admit it. They passed the spot by the log, where they had been when Scoop surprised them, but there was no sign of the dog. They were hustled along roughly by the two men, across the dam—in the starlight, for night had arrived—and then into the brush on the other side of the river. In another few moments, they reached the haunted house. It was as dark as pitch. They were pushed through a door and pulled along a dark hallway. Then they stood there, with Itchy holding fast to them, while Scoop went through another door, where a light showed briefly as he opened it and disappeared inside. They heard voices then, low at first but growing louder and sharper.

Suddenly the door flew open, and Scoop stood there.

"Bring 'em in," he said, hoarser than ever.

The children were pushed, stumbling, into a large room with an old couch and several chairs in it. There were heavy drapes covering the windows, so no light could be seen from the outside, and there at a table sat Mr. Geyser, his long, pale face and glittering eyes turned toward them.

"Mr. Geyser," said Carlyle instantly, "I don't think your friends are very polite."

"Never mind, Carly," Cam told her. "Don't say anything. Don't talk."

"Now, dere's a really wise kid," Scoop growled sarcastically.

"Shut your trap," Geyser said, without moving his lips. "These kids are friends of mine. Now, you kids sit down here, and we'll have a little talk. We'll have a little talk about a box you took out of the river, that's all. We just want to make sure where you left it, so we can get it, and then you can go home and see your nice father and mother. And until we find the box, you aren't going home to see your nice father and mother—ever. Now, let's hear the real truth. Where's the box?"

Cam drew a deep breath and looked squarely at

Mr. Geyser, who was watching him intently.

"I threw it in the river," he said.

Geyser showed a bit of his teeth.

"You threw it in the river. Are you sure?"

"I heard it hit the water."

"So did I," said Carlyle.

"I heard sump'n hit da water," Itchy said, scratching his head. "Coulda been it."

"You could dive for it," said Cam. "I showed Mr. Itchy right where we were when I threw it."

"You're being helpful," said Mr. Geyser, "but you probably don't realize that we don't have time to cover the whole river bottom. Now, Cam and Carlyle, my boys are out searching the woods and the river. It's very important that they find that box. I'm going to keep you here for a while, until they come back with the box. If they don't find it very soon, I just don't think we'll be able to let you go at all. It's a shame, I know, but kids ought to stay out of trouble and not get nosy."

"I'm very sorry," said Cam, "but I threw it in the river because I got scared."

"So, you little brat, you got scared, did you?" Geyser barked, beginning to forget his fine language. "You got scared! Now, shut up for a while. Nose-Job—" he motioned to a thin young fellow leaning against the nearby wall—"you keep an eye on these two. I gotta make that phone call. Scoop and Itchy, go help the boys. I gotta real nice bonus for the guy that finds it first." He looked at his watch. "We got one hour. That's all."

The three walked out, and the children were left with the thin young man. Cam and Carlyle sat still on the wooden bench by the table, close together. Nose-Job took Geyser's chair and stretched his legs. He had a long face with bumps on it, but the remarkable thing about him was his nose. It was not only too large for his face, but also, when it came to the tip, it turned, very suddenly, as though whoever had been sculpturing it had been startled at that moment and had pushed it accidentally.

"One peep outta youse squoits," said the owner of the nose, "an' I'll tie y'z up so tight y'z wouldn' be able ta sneeze." He sat there looking at them for a moment and then began tapping his fingers on the table. Then he took out a cigarette and lit it. The children were silent, trying not to stare but not succeeding.

"Quit givin' me da eye an' shuddup," growled Nose-Job, although they hadn't said a word. Then Carlyle raised a hand. Nose-Job paid no attention. On his youthful face lay the triumphant sneer of the successful gangster. Carlyle held her hand higher and waved it a little.

"Whassat fer?" said Nose-Job. "Watcha doin'?"

"I just wanted to ask you something," Carlyle

answered timidly, her eyes fixed on him.

"Never mind, Carly," said her brother.

"But I only wanted to ask him why—"

"Shuddup!" Nose-Job said fiercely. "Quit y'r yowlin', hear me?"

Carlyle pressed her lips together and said nothing. The young man took a pack of cards out of a drawer and began to play solitaire. There was silence again. Suddenly he looked up.

"*Now* whatcha starin' at?"

"I only wanted to ask you why—" began Carlyle, and then she stopped, taking a deep breath. Nose-Job threw down the cards and jumped up. He began to walk about the room, muttering to himself about baby-sitters, nursemaids, and always getting the raw end of a deal. Then he stopped and glared at the little girl.

"Whatcha wanna ast me—why *what?*" he demanded, his eyes narrowing.

"I wanted to ask you why they call you . . . that," said Carlyle.

"Call me what?"

"Mr. . . . Mr. Nose-Job."

"Dey don't 'zackly call me *Mister.* Dey call me Nose-Job cuz it's my name."

"You mean your mother *named* you that?"

Nose-Job gave her one startled look and slapped his hand down on the table, grabbing at the cards lying there. At the same time, he uttered a hoarse cry of pain and pulled back his hand.

"Ow! Ow! Ow!" he cried, shaking his fingers, and the children could see a bright drop of scarlet that had dripped onto the tabletop. Nose-Job took out a handkerchief and held it to his injured finger, then drew it off, examining the finger carefully to see if it was still bleeding.

"What happened?" asked Carlyle.

"Gotta piece uh da table up my nail—'bout t'ree inches woit'," he exaggerated, with a deep groan. He mopped at it again, and then, after studying the wound for a long minute from every possible angle, he commenced with an attempt to extricate the splinter with his right hand. The children watched him, absorbed in what he was doing. They had never seen anyone fumble so clumsily in trying to remove a splinter—or with such dirty hands. When they had splinters, Mother had them wash their hands well, used tweezers to remove the splinter, and then applied antiseptic.

Nose-Job, muttering to himself, mopping at his finger, and making horrible faces as he worked at the splinter, knew they were watching him.

"So I'm a sout'paw," he exclaimed angrily. "I can't git no splinter out wit' my right hand. I'm left-handed."

"We'd be glad to help you," said Carlyle.

"Youse set tight!" he snapped. There was a long silence while he fumbled and perspired, the children watching.

"I once knew a man," said Cam, his voice sounding loud in the half-empty room, "who got a splinter in his finger and bled to death."

"Yeah," said Nose-Job.

"In fifteen minutes," said Cam. "He didn't even realize it. He just died."

"Yeah, I c'n bleeve dat," jeered Nose-Job.

"Oh, you don't believe me?" Cam asked. "But it's true. He had something wrong with his blood that he didn't know about. It wouldn't coagulate. He was dead in fifteen minutes."

After a moment, Carlyle said, "Remember the man who lived next door to us in Wisconsin? Mr. Linny?"

"Yes," said Cam, though they had never lived anywhere near Wisconsin and had been out of California only once, "I remember poor Mr. Linny. That was awful."

Nose-Job stopped scraping at his finger. "Yeah?" he said. "Wha' happened to 'im?"

"He got a splinter in his finger, and it got infected. He was dead in the morning. Stone-dead."

"From a *splinter?*" Nose-Job's eyebrows shot upward in disbelief.

"It was from a dirty wooden table," said Carlyle,

"like this one. He got septicemia. Poor Mr. Linny; he was so nice. He looked a lot like you, Mr. Nose-Job."

"Now, look here, youse kids," said Nose-Job, "youse quit spookin' me wit' dem wisecracks. . . ."

"We just want to help you, Mr. Nose-Job," Carlyle said in her most motherly voice. "Infection can be very dangerous."

"More people die from infections than from . . . uh . . . appendectomies," Cam ventured, with a deep sigh.

Nose-Job threw down the knife he was using.

"Fry me a egg!" he spluttered. "Youse kids gotta quit spookin' me! Shut y'r traps, or I'll shut 'em fer y'z, hear?" He held his finger up to the light and scowled at it, turning it this way and that.

"Is it hot?" Carlyle asked solicitously.

"Whatcha mean—hot?"

"Does it throb?"

Nose-Job felt his wounded finger tenderly, frowning horribly. "I dunno." He felt it again.

"Touch it to your forehead," Carlyle urged. "If it feels hot, then . . . then I'm afraid it's infected."

"Ya mean ya c'n tell dat way?" He put his finger to his forehead and left it there, his mouth hanging open in concentration.

"Yeah—" he breathed heavily—"yeah, it sure does. It feels hot. *Gosh*."

"Whew!" Cam shook his head. "That's the worst sign. And it happened so fast!"

"Oh, Mr. Nose-Job," Carlyle said, "you'd better get some medicine on that *fast!*"

"How come—" Nose-Job gulped, his face turning paler—"how come youse kids know so much 'bout dem t'ings—septy . . . septy . . . whatever youse wuz talkin' 'bout?"

"Septicemia," Cam said. Then he added, with serious finality, "Our father is a doctor, you see."

"Oh, yeah?"

"We've even helped him on cases," Carlyle said modestly. "You know, emergencies, where he had to treat people right away and not a soul was around. Like that."

"Dat's how come youse know 'bout it bein' hot an' holdin' it ta y'r forehead an' all dat?"

Carlyle nodded. "You learn so much, living right in the same house with a doctor. If poor Mr. Linny had only called Father—" She broke off with a sigh.

"He didn' call 'im or *nuttin'?*" asked Nose-Job. "An' he lived right nex' door? Whatta dumb cluck." He was staring at his finger uneasily.

"Just like you," Cam said, as if all were lost, "he didn't know about septicemia. Poor Mr. Linny."

The children both sighed and then were silent, thinking about Mr. Linny.

Nose-Job stared at them, his lips pursed; then he

touched his finger to his forehead again, growing three shades paler. He stood up. "Youse kids don't move, now, hear?" He went to the door. "Sniffer!" he called. "Hey, Sniff!" He stood there, looking at his finger anxiously, but there was no answer. Stepping out into the hall, he called again, holding on to the doorknob of the half-opened door.

9
The Plight Worsens

The children looked at each other and read each other's thoughts. Cam shook his head.

"I think the window's open behind the drapes," he whispered, "but we couldn't get out before he saw us."

"It's open," Carlyle whispered back. "I saw the drapes move with the wind."

Nose-Job came back into the room, his face a picture of misery.

"Dey're leavin' me ta die up here alone, dat's what dey're doin'," he muttered, glaring at the children as if they were to blame.

"I'm sorry we said anything," Cam told him, his voice full of sympathy, "but we thought you ought to know. You might *still* be able to save yourself if you have it amputated."

"That's right," Carlyle said eagerly. "That's what Father would say."

"Youse mean *cut my finger off?*" Nose-Job looked horrified.

"Not now," Cam said. "It's too late. We mean your whole hand."

"Maybe your arm, if you don't hurry," Carlyle added.

Nose-Job gave them one dreadful look and bolted out the door. They could hear him in the hallway, bellowing loudly for Sniffer.

The children, staring at the window, saw the drapes move and then part a little. A furry, black and white nose and curly chin whiskers suddenly appeared, and after them came a pair of bright black eyes.

"Tee-Bo!" The children started to run toward him.

"Get back! Sit down!" Tee-Bo hissed. "Don't give me away! I don't want another conk on the bean!" He put his forepaws on the sill and shoved his head farther through the window.

"Who hit you?" Cam whispered indignantly.

"That character called Scoop," Tee-Bo said, "laid

me out with a rap of his gun, back there on the path. Do you notice that I am beginning to talk just like a gangster?"

"Oh, Tee-Bo," Carlyle said, "are you all right?"

"A trifle dizzy," he admitted, "but it's nothing. Now, I want to tell you something. If Nose-Job comes back, I'll duck and you look the other way. *Don't try to run.* Don't try to get away. I'll get you out of here in no time, but you have to let *me* tell you when."

"Why don't you get Father to call the police?" Cam asked. "Carlyle and I don't like these people."

"I like Mr. Nose-Job," Carlyle said.

"I went back to the cottage," said Tee-Bo, "but your mother and father had gone to the sheriff's office. I don't know what's happening now. I had to get up here to see if you were all right. Are you sure you are?"

"Yes, but why can't we get out the window now?" Cam asked.

"You'd run right into one of the boys," Tee-Bo said, "and in the dark, they just might shoot first and ask questions afterward. I know what I'm doing. You two stay put and don't be scared. If I can get your father and the sheriff, I will."

"Couldn't you bring them here, Tee-Bo, and show them where we are?" Carlyle said eagerly.

"You want to be in a big shoot-out?" Tee-Bo

asked. "These fellows are playing for keeps. Besides," he added, his chin whiskers bristling, "whenever I try to tell your parents anything important, your father gives me water and your mother feeds me. Anyway," he went on, "this is a case where we have to outwit Francis the First."

"Who's Francis the First?" Carlyle asked.

"That's Call-Me-Francis himself, one of America's hindmost third-class petty crooks, known to the law and to the world of crime in general as Francis the First. I've been listening in while they searched the river."

"Oh, for the box!" the children said together.

"The one Cam threw in the river."

"Oh, I didn't really—"

"Don't say another word!" interrupted Tee-Bo. "What I don't know won't hurt me! I'm going to get help. Now, I'll be back, and don't you two worry!"

"Be careful!" the children cautioned.

"One more thing," Tee-Bo said, thrusting his nose back through the drapes. "Maybe you'd better tell—"

He didn't finish, for, at that moment, Nose-Job opened the door and rushed in, hunched over in pain and holding his wrist. Where Tee-Bo's nose had been, the drapes moved gently, as if from the summer breeze.

"How are you feeling, Mr. Nose-Job?" asked Carlyle.

"Shuddup!" answered Nose-Job rudely. He sat down at the table, holding his finger up to the light. His shoulders shook, and beads of perspiration stood out on his forehead.

"Dey don't care nuttin' 'bout me!" he said, sounding as if he might suddenly burst into tears. "Dey don't care if I die or get a arm cut off or nuttin'! Anyways, we gotta move out pretty quick, no matter what, an' I'm goin' straight ta a doc. I don't care what nobody says; it's *my* arm, ain't it?"

"You're leaving?" Cam asked.

"Yeah, on accounta youse dumb kids." Nose-Job sniffed loudly and then glared reproachfully at them. "If youse hadn' did watcha done, we'd a been gone, an' I might notta got myself hoit. Youse done us all up good an' proper, an' da boss ain't gonna fergit it, neither. A fine paira kids youse are!"

Just then Sniffer poked his head around the open door. "Hey, Nose-Job."

"Yeah."

"Ya ready?"

"Ready? Sure, I'm ready. What's doin'?"

"We're pullin' out inna few secs. Da river's crawlin'. Dey'll be up here pretty quick, we figger."

"Did Francis say I could see a doc? Didja ast 'im, like I said?"

"Ya nuts or sump'n?" Sniffer asked. "Ya ain't gonna see no doc!"

"Den I'm gonna die," wailed poor Nose-Job, turning greener than ever. "Whadda buncha bums; whadda rotten buncha bums! Hoo-hoo-hoo!"

"Aw, shuddup, will ya?" Sniffer snarled. "Look, da boss wants ya should—" he gestured—"you know, take care a da brats an' den git outside, on da double."

"Me?" asked Nose-Job, raising his head and looking shocked.

"Yeah, *you.*"

"I ain't in no shape, I tell ya!" Nose-Job protested. "I'm real sick! Ya gotta tell 'im!"

"Nose-Job," Sniffer said, shaking his head back and forth, "y're gittin' me mad, an' y're gittin' da boss mad. Now, ya got ten minutes. Dat's it."

The children looked at each other soberly but said nothing.

Nose-Job stretched his hand out on the table and surveyed it mournfully. "I ain't in no shape ta do no job!" he declared. "An' him not even lettin' me see no doc! How long didja say it took dat dere Mr. Linny ta die? Da one y'r ole man didn' take care of?"

"Oh, just a few hours!" Cam replied.

"He was dead in the morning, you know," Carlyle added.

"Yeah." Nose-Job heaved a sigh and stared at his useless finger.

Cam drew a big breath. "Mr. Nose-Job, there *is* something you can do for your finger, and maybe you won't even have to have it amputated."

"Yeah?" said Nose-Job quickly. "Ya mean it?"

"I'm just beginning to remember another . . . case—" pause— "of my father's, where he saved a man's life—"

"Oh," said Carlyle, "you mean the time that man came to his office late at night when it was raining? Last winter?"

"That's the one," Cam answered. "He had run a splinter under his nail, just like you did, and then hadn't done anything for it, and he was in pretty bad shape. Just about like you are now, Mr. Nose-Job."

"So wha'd y'r ole man do?"

"I'm trying to remember." Cam frowned and looked up at the ceiling. "He did something for him —in a hurry, too—and it saved him."

"He didn' hafta have nuttin' cut off?"

"No, not even his finger. He did *something*, if only I can remember."

"Maybe a liddle medicine he had?" Nose-Job inquired hopefully.

"No." Carlyle shook her head. "I remember Father saying that no medicine could save him. . . ."

"Youse wuz dere, too?" asked poor Nose-Job pitifully, perhaps taking comfort in numbers.

"We were both there," Carlyle said. "We were helping him."

"I think I'm getting it . . ." Cam said. He stopped as Sniffer stuck his head in the doorway.

"Ya got 'bout five minutes. What's keepin' ya? Da boss keeps askin'!"

"Be out inna jiff," Nose-Job said, but his eyes were far away, and he was not even thinking of what he was saying. "Yeah, kid," he urged, "wha'd y'r ole man do? Come on!"

"I've got it!" Cam cried brightly. "Remember, Carly? He cut it out with his knife first, and then he put . . . he put—"

"Tobacco all over it, out of a cigarette!"

"That's right! And the tobacco worked as . . . as an aphorism—"

"Or analgesic," Carlyle offered helpfully.

"Yes, both of them!" Cam said triumphantly. "And it drew out all the poison and saved him!"

"Just in time, too." Carlyle nodded, adding gravely, "Mr. Nose-Job, you'd better give Cam your knife."

"Y're not gonna cut no hole in my finger!" cried Nose-Job, breathing hard.

"Oh"—Cam looked at him solicitously—"just a small hole."

"Look, kid, dat's my *finger* yer talkin' 'bout! I *use* dat finger, like fer pointin' an' stuff like dat. How much good it's gonna be wit' a chunk sliced outta it?"

"Mr. Nose-Job"—Cam's voice was gentle—"how much good will your finger be if you're dead?"

Uttering a high, thin wail, Nose-Job, by now a broken man, handed over his knife.

10
The Real Racer

When Tee-Bo left the children alone in the room with Nose-Job, he knew the situation was desperate. Francis the First's boys had been searching the woods and the river for the lost box, but, with the sheriff's men out hunting for the missing children, they had been forced to retire quietly and would have to get out of the old house in a hurry if they were not to be caught. Tee-Bo had seen the big black car primed for a getaway, and, sneaking through the woods past it, to find the children, he had heard enough to make his chin whiskers curl. There was no time to be lost.

"I can't bring Father up to the big house; he'd be shot at," Tee-Bo determined. "And I can't lead the sheriff there, either, while the children are there." He sighed. "No, this has to be a one-man job, and it has to be a mighty quick one, and there's only one person who can do it."

So he kept to the shadows and moved furtively over the grounds without being seen. Once on the highway, he raced for the village faster than he had ever run before. He even passed a highway patrolman on a motorcycle, going the same way, who was so astonished that he lost his goggles.

Through the town and straight to a small cabin he raced, his heart pounding. Good! A light was on, so someone was there. He bounded up the stairs and scratched at the door, whining and barking.

After a moment the door was opened, and Larry Blade stood there, a puzzled look on his face. Then he saw Tee-Bo.

"Tee-Bo!" he exclaimed, bending over and hugging and pounding him gently. "Where've you been? Where are the kids?"

"Racer," said Tee-Bo, trembling with eagerness, "if you've ever used your wits, please ask them to do double duty now. Try to understand what I'm saying. Try!"

"You've got a nasty bump on your head, old fella," said young Mr. Blade. "I'd give a million bucks if you could tell me where you've been."

"I'd give a million bucks if you'd just listen," said Tee-Bo, panting hard in a very frenzy of worry and concern.

"Wait a minute," said Blade. "Stay, boy. Don't go away."

He walked back into the room and picked up a telephone, having been interrupted in the middle of a conversation, and from the look on his face and the tone of his voice, Tee-Bo could tell it was a very special call.

"Chief," said Racer in a low voice, "the kids' dog just walked in.... Yeah, I'm sure. I know him. He's been hurt—has a bad bump on his head—which just about verifies what we were discussing. I'm sure now that it's Francis the First.... Yes, I will, if I can get him to. I'll have to go alone.... I know. ... Even if it means exposing my identity, I've got to get those kids.... Right; there's no time to put on another man.... Right. Okay."

He put down the phone and looked at Tee-Bo. "Fella," he said grimly, "you've *got* to take me to those kids, understand?"

"Oh, forevermore!" cried Tee-Bo, in the same tones that Mother used in a crisis. "Get your gun and let's go!"

He ran to the door, whining and growling as he pushed against it.

"Okay, okay!" Racer grabbed his jacket and started to follow.

"Your gun!" Tee-Bo yelled at him. "Get your gun, chowderhead!"

"Just a minute," said Blade. "I'll get my gun." He strapped it on under his jacket and opened the door.

Tee-Bo was out like a streak, only the whites of his eyes showing as he looked back to see if Blade was following. It was only a ten-minute walk to the haunted house, but he knew they had to make it in half that time. Blade soon understood exactly where the dog was headed and doubled his speed.

"Good for you, boy!" he panted, running beside Tee-Bo. "Go on, go on!"

"Lucky for us that I suspected you from the first, Mr. Undercover Agent," Tee-Bo flung out as they ran, "though I'll never know why you told those phony stories about having a quarrel with your wife."

Tee-Bo slowed down when they reached the big gates at the front entrance. Here there was a grove of redwoods, with a long, curving driveway leading to the house. This was the driveway the getaway car would take.

"Easy does it," warned Tee-Bo, taking a jog to the left and bypassing the gate. "From here on in, one false move and you're dead. Francis the First's boys are scattered all over the place like buckshot."

Blade jogged a little to the left and followed, moving cautiously, one hand on his holster.

"Good boy, Tee-Bo," he murmured. "Easy does it! Francis the First's boys are probably planted out here in rows, like corn."

"Like I said," Tee-Bo agreed.

They proceeded toward the house in the dark. Floodlights and torches blazed across the river, and they could hear the faint cries of the searching party. The big house was dark, and it looked empty. Tee-Bo's heart leaped and then seemed to stick in his throat. There was a low, steady roar coming from the driveway, where the big black car was parked. Its motor was running and its headlights were on. Several shadowy figures hunched together inside the car.

Tee-Bo let out a yelp and bounded ahead.

"It's now or never, old boy!" he cried, and, throwing caution to the winds, he made a beeline for the side of the house where the children had been imprisoned, running zigzag well behind the black car and praying that Blade would not be seen.

Racer was right after him, light as a cat, barely making a sound, but the occupants of the car had seen him, and there was a loud crackling and snapping roar as gunfire echoed and reechoed through the night air.

"This way!" cried Tee-Bo, trembling so that he could hardly speak, and he jumped right through the open window, the drapes swishing as he passed. Blade was right on his heels, bending over and running toward the window.

"Tee-Bo!" cried the children as he bounced down on the floor beside them and dived, with a growl, at Nose-Job.

"Stop!" cried the children. "Be careful!"

"Git 'im offa me!" screamed Nose-Job helplessly.

"Whatever in the world are you doing?" Tee-Bo demanded, backing off in disbelief as he saw Cam holding tight to Nose-Job's hand and brandishing a knife over it.

"I'm performing a small operation," Cam replied with dignity.

At that very moment, Racer Blade stepped in through the window, his gun out of its holster and pointed straight at Nose-Job.

"All right, you," he said, "put your gun on the table—easy—and back up against the wall. On the double!"

"Why, Mr. Blade!" both children said at once. Carlyle added quickly, "Don't shoot Mr. Nose-Job! He's not at all well."

"I'm a dyin' man," said poor Nose-Job, who had put his gun down and was backing dutifully against the wall, holding out his sore finger awkwardly.

"Don't move, Nose-Job," Blade said, rather soft-ly, but his eyes were the color of gunshot now—no longer friendly.

"We were about to sprinkle tobacco on his cut," Cam explained carefully, pointing to a small pile of tobacco lying in a mound on one of Nose-Job's cigarette papers. Blade looked somewhat startled, but his eyes were riveted on the unhappy culprit sagging against the wall.

"I didn't know you had a gun, Mr. Blade," Car-lyle said. The words were hardly spoken, when there was a sound of running footsteps outside the door.

"Uh-oh! Under the table, quick! Here comes trouble!" cried Tee-Bo.

"Quick! Under the table, kids!" Blade barked out his orders, and just as the children sprawled on the floor, the door burst open, and Mr. Geyser lunged into the room, followed by his boys. Scoop, Sniffer, and Itchy were among them.

"Looks like the trap fell into the bait, now, doesn't it?" sneered Geyser, leveling his gun at Mr. Blade. "Now, just give your gun to Scoop, here, nice and easy. We're getting out of here, and we'll take the kids to make sure we aren't stopped. Nose-Job, as a reward for doing your duty, which you failed to do, we'll just leave you here to keep this chap com-pany—and in the same condition, so you won't be

jealous of each other." He chuckled, then jerked his head toward Sniffer. "Get the kids and pile them into the car. I'll take care of these two. Get going!"

As Sniffer moved toward the children, Tee-Bo jumped at him, sinking his teeth firmly into his outstretched hand. Sniffer, jerking backward as if he had been shot out of a cannon, crashed straight into Geyser, who was behind him, knocking Geyser's gun out of his hand and hitting him so hard that both men landed on the floor, arms and legs tangled. Almost at the same instant, the hallway outside was filled with strange men, who seemed to be pouring in from all sides, while more entered through the window. All carried guns and wore badges.

There was a brief period of frightful confusion, during which Geyser and Sniffer were untangled and miraculously handcuffed and lined up against the wall, amid grunts and groans and threats and a general shuffling of feet and other noises.

"Sheriff Gurgle," said Racer Blade, when some of the confusion had abated, "your timing was almost as good as Tee-Bo's. My thanks."

"And who might you be?" asked the sheriff, not at all friendly. Blade stepped up and pulled open his jacket. The sheriff's face at once broke into smiles, and his voice became hearty.

"Well, sir!" he boomed out, shaking the other's

hand up and down, like a pump handle. "Who would have thought it! And such a young feller, too!"

"Oh, I'm older than I look," Blade replied modestly as he tried to reclaim his hand.

"May we come out from under the table now?" Carlyle called politely, not having wanted to interrupt before.

"Great radishes!" cried the sheriff, bending down and beaming at them, his face red as he doubled up. "Your parents are in the lower field with some of my men, half out of their wits! Gadby! Gadby!" He turned to a deputy. "Get Dr. and Mrs. McRae and bring them here. Tell 'em the kids are okay."

The children were led from the house by the sheriff, followed by Racer Blade, with Tee-Bo bounding along beside them.

"Good boy, Tee-Bo, good fella!" Racer kept saying, over and over. "You saved us all; you really did. You're a hero!"

"He'll have me stuffed with conceit," declared Tee-Bo, looking as if he enjoyed it immensely.

"You mean overstuffed," Cam told him.

"Weren't you scared, Tee-Bo?" Carlyle asked.

"I was petrified," Tee-Bo said solemnly, "just petrified."

Everyone walked through the doorway and to the front of the house. The big black car still stood there, lights off and motor silent. Sheriff Gurgle had

Geyser and his boys to one side, surrounded by deputies. They looked dejected and sullen, now that they were disarmed and taken into custody. Suddenly there was a happy shout, and Father and Mother came running up the path from behind the house.

"I don't know why I'm crying," said Mother, wiping her eyes with Father's handkerchief, "but it seems to be a g-good idea . . . oh, boo-hoo-hoo. . . ." She went on crying and hugging the children, while Father did the same thing, only without tears, and the sheriff and his men looked on with solemn faces. One or two of them swallowed rather noisily.

"We're quite all right, you know," Cam insisted, for the twelfth time.

"It was rather exciting," Carlyle said, "except when Tee-Bo got hurt. That was awful."

"I was knocked out flat," Tee-Bo declared.

"We'll have to see about that bump on your head," Blade decided, patting him, and everyone began talking at the same time, each one explaining carefully exactly what had happened and no two telling the same story.

Father began shaking hands. "We want to thank you, Sheriff Gargle."

"Gurgle," said the sheriff, beaming.

"Gurgle," repeated Father, nodding. "You performed your duty manfully."

Gurgle looked self-conscious, his face pinker than ever. "I guess the law has been trying to nab this here Francis the First for about two years now, ever since he pulled that Bliffy job and got away with the Bliffy diamonds. Almost a million dollars in diamonds. Some haul!"

"Consternation!" gulped Tee-Bo. "Do you suppose that was what was in the *box?*"

"Dr. McRae," the sheriff said in his booming voice, "we'd be honored to drive you and your family home now. Reckon you're pretty tired."

As he finished speaking, there was a sudden stir and a small commotion from the band of captured men. One of them tried to push forward but was restrained by a deputy.

"Hoo-hoo-hoo," moaned an unhappy voice, "I'm a dyin' man, I am, an' a doc oughtta see me quick!"

11
The Contents of the Box

Tee-Bo rolled his eyes as the sniffling grew louder. "Will that fellow never quit?"

"Oh, it's poor Mr. Nose-Job!" Carlyle exclaimed in sympathy. "He has a splinter in his finger."

"What?" said Father, as if he had not heard her right.

"I was performing an operation on him when we were interrupted," Cam explained. "You see," he added, because everyone was staring at him, "I'm a doctor's son."

"Oh?" Father said. "Are you?" He walked over to where poor Nose-Job was whimpering, begging to see a doctor while there was still time.

"Whatever ails you?" Father asked curiously but politely.

Nose-Job held out his finger with the splinter.

"Dey wuz takin' care of it real good, like ya told 'em, Doc, but da job ain't done, an' I might die," he blubbered.

"From what," asked Father, squinting at the finger in the torchlight, "dirt?"

"I might get septy . . . septy-sump'n from it." Nose-Job wailed louder than ever.

"Septicemia," Cam offered, not looking at Father.

"You might try soap and water," Father suggested coolly.

"But dey wuz gonna cut it open an' sprinkle ter-bakker on it, like ya said ta do!"

"Like *I* said!"

Nose-Job squinted up at him, scowling fearfully.

"Ain't ya da kids' ole man?"

"I am their father."

"Ain't ya da doc?"

"Yes, a professor of history," Father replied, "but that hardly qualifies me to remove a splinter. Mrs. McRae is far more experienced at that than I."

But Nose-Job, scowling more horribly than ever, wasn't to be put off that easily.

"But what happened ta all dem people ya took care of, wit' da kids helpin'? An' what 'bout poor

Mr. Linny? An' dat feller who died in fifteen minutes from a splinter'n *his* finger? What 'bout dem guys, huh?"

"Why, yes," Father said, turning toward the children, "what about Mr. Linny?"

"Mr. *Who?*" asked Cam.

"Mr. Linny?" repeated Carlyle, wrinkling her nose as if exerting every effort to remember. "I never heard of a Mr. Linny, did you, Cam?"

"No," Cam said, "never."

"*Never?*" exploded Nose-Job, dabbing at his eyes with his fist. "Youse never hoid 'bout poor Mr. Linny who lived next door ta y'z in Wisconsin an' who wouldn'a died from a splinter if he'd got ta y'r ole man foist? Huh? Ya *never?*"

"Yes," said Father, more curious than ever, "what about that?"

The children shook their heads politely.

"We've never been to Wisconsin," they said.

"True." Father nodded. "They haven't. Not ever."

Here Nose-Job let out a yowl that echoed through the night air and was heard clear on the other side of the river and as far away as Rio Nido. Carlyle walked over to him, waiting until he had quieted down somewhat.

"Mr. Nose-Job," she said in a motherly way, "the nurse at the police station will wash your hands with soap and water and take out the splinter with a pair of tweezers, and you'll be as fit as a fiddle. So don't worry. You won't die. We just told you that so we could keep you from doing what Mr. Geyser—I mean, Francis the First—told Sniffer to tell you to do to us. You know." She drew one finger across her throat, rolling her eyes with an exaggerated gesture of explanation.

Father opened his mouth to shush her, then thought better of it and patted Mother's arm instead—which was a wise decision.

They were all piling into the sheriff's station wagon, when Cam had a thought.

"Couldn't we walk back over the dam and take the river path home? There's something Carly and I'd like to show you—and the sheriff."

Both parents said it was late, but if he could persuade the sheriff to do it, they would go along, too. "But only, mind you," Father added, "with Sheriff Gaggle's permission."

"Gargle," Cam said. "I mean, *Gurgle.*"

He walked over to where the sheriff was giving last-minute instructions to his deputies.

"Well, young man," boomed the sheriff, "come to say good night?"

"Not yet," Cam replied politely. "Sheriff Gar . . . Gur . . . gle, if you and your men and Mr. Geyser— I mean, Francis the First—and his boys will follow my parents and my sister and me—"

"And me, too," Tee-Bo put in, his ears bouncing as he followed at Cam's side.

"And Tee-Bo," Cam added, "we can show you something that will surprise you."

"Out of your living wits," Tee-Bo added.

"*Tonight?*" asked the sheriff.

"Right now," Cam said firmly.

"A surprise," said Carlyle, coming up behind her brother. "A great big, indescribable one—we think."

"You want all of us to follow you—my prisoners and my deputies, too?" repeated the sheriff, who was somewhat hardheaded.

"Just across the dam, then back to the village along the river road instead of the highway. It won't take long."

"It might help us all to sleep, at that," Mother said as she and Father joined them. "A warm night and a quiet walk before bed—sounds nice."

"It might even prove interesting," Father said, giving Cam a strange look.

"I had the same thought myself," said Racer Blade.

"Well, if you approve, Dr. McRae," the sheriff said resignedly. His boots were new and tight, and his gun was heavy, but he was still excited about capturing a crook as important as Francis the First, so he wasn't really ready for bed yet, either.

Accordingly, the sheriff lined up his prisoners, with deputies on all sides. Mother and Father walked behind the children, and Cameron and Carlyle took the lead, with Mr. Blade at their side and Tee-Bo following. In this formation, they started down the bank to cross the dam to the other side of the river.

The moment they started, Carlyle began chatting with Mr. Blade.

"I was certainly surprised to find that you were a policeman, too," she said, looking up at him in a way that told him there was much more to come.

"I think it was a surprise all around," he admitted boyishly, "with one exception, perhaps. . . ."

"That would be me," Tee-Bo said proudly.

"Ahem!" Father, who had heard all this, cleared his throat and looked self-conscious, while he and Mother exchanged glances.

"Oh, no!" Tee-Bo cried, with great exasperation.

"We were not *too* sure," Father admitted, "but it added up; it added up!"

"Yeah, one and one makes three," put in Tee-Bo, with killing sarcasm.

"*Tee*-Bo—" began Carlyle.

"Well, Father is always stealing my thunder. After all, who went after Blade?"

"How did you know Mr. Blade was a special investigator?" Cam asked, forgetting himself.

"It was simple," the dog answered. "I used my canine instincts. Besides, I'm a great student of human behaviorism."

"Now you sound like Father," Cam muttered.

"Sometimes I almost believe that Tee-Bo talks to the children," Mother said, shaking her head. "Sometimes it sounds just as if they're carrying on a conversation."

"Your mother," Tee-Bo stated, "is a doll. A living doll."

"But, Mr. Blade," Carlyle went on, "what about your wife? Won't she be proud of you, now that you've captured Francis the First?"

"Well, kids"—Mr. Blade's nice, smooth skin turned faintly pink—"I have to apologize for that. I told you that story because I needed to have a reason for being here. A man vacationing alone would have looked suspicious to the gang. So I . . . I made up that story. Please forgive me."

"And you didn't have a quarrel with your wife?"

"I'm not even married," he said, blushing pinker.

"Carlyle," said Mother.

"Oh, no, that's all right," Larry Blade insisted, grinning and blushing still. "You see, I was an undercover agent for a long time, and I couldn't get married. Nobody knew me, and I was a valuable man. But now the story's out. Every crook from here to Istanbul will know me, so I'm taking a new job. Also, I'm going to get married—next week, if possible!"

"Isn't that awfully fast?" asked Carlyle.

"Carlyle!" said Mother again.

"I don't think so," beamed Mr. Blade. "We've known each other ever since we went to school, back in Wisconsin."

"Are you sure she waited for you, Mr. Blade?" asked Carlyle worriedly.

"Carlyle!" Mother and Father said together.

"Yes," declared Racer Blade happily, "and she will be just as glad as I am that I'm quitting my old job!"

"Another good man down the drain," said Tee-Bo, but no one heard him, for they had crossed the dam and were approaching the spot where the old rowboat lay, one end half-submerged in the water.

"Everybody wait here," said Cam, "and Carlyle and I will show you something."

They all stopped and waited, Francis the First and his boys looking sullen, and Sheriff Gurgle standing first on one foot and then on the other, shifting his holster from time to time. Nose-Job was holding his manacled hands up and had asked Itchy to look at his finger in the beam of the search-light.

The children ran down to the water's edge and returned a moment later, Cam holding the box aloft for everyone to see. There was silence for a whole half minute, and then came great shouts of surprise from all sides.

Sheriff Gurgle stepped up, and Cam put the box in his hands. The sheriff took a knife from his pocket and pried open the lid. Everyone crowded around to see.

There lay a string of diamonds, glittering like fire in the torchlight!

"The Bliffy diamonds!" howled Sheriff Gurgle, forgetting that his feet hurt. "They *are* the Bliffy stones, aren't they, Blade?"

Blade, ex-undercover agent, bent over and took a long look.

"The same," said he, in an awed voice, "and the end of a long, long search!"

The sheriff let out a low whistle. "A million dollars in rocks!"

Silence fell over everyone as he said this, for very few people there had ever seen a million dollars in diamonds fished out of a half-sunken rowboat by a little boy and girl at midnight—or by anyone else at any other place or at any other time, for that matter.

"Why," said Mother, breaking the deep silence, "I thought the children were— How on earth could they do all this so secretly?"

Now a loud wail came from the tail end of the

group, and Francis the First, with a wild look in his eye, said loudly, "Those kids were fooling me all the time, and I swallowed it, hook, line, and sinker!" He was so angry that the gnashing of his teeth could be heard from several yards away.

Of course, everyone began praising the children, and Sheriff Gurgle patted their heads and promised them a reward. Then he told Mother and Father how proud he was to know the parents of such enterprising children and things like that, but Cam and Carlyle began to speak up quite loudly and firmly, saying that it was Tee-Bo, their dog, who had discovered the box first.

"Forevermore," said Tee-Bo, "I thought you'd never get around to me!"

So then he was patted and praised and called a "good dog" and a "brave fellow," until his eyes were rolling in his head.

But suddenly Father looked at him. "Tee-Bo," he said sternly, "you may be a hero and all that, but just suppose there had been a *bomb* in that box!"

"Forevermore!" exclaimed Tee-Bo. "What a way to show your gratitude!" He was so put out, he forgot that no one but the children could hear him.

"Don't worry," they said. "You know Father."

"I do indeed," replied Tee-Bo, "so well that I needn't look far to get even with *him*."

Which is why, when newspaper photographers

from miles around appeared the next day and took their pictures—as the heroes in the Bliffy diamonds recovery—Dr. McRae, though otherwise neatly dressed, was barefoot, and the mongrel dog standing between the two children looked for all the world as if he were laughing.